"From this moment on, this night is about what you want. So what's it going to be, Gina?"

Justin leaned in, knowing he shouldn't touch her, but still he ran the tip of his finger along her jaw.

"I want to dance."

He straightened. "You want to what?"

"I want to dance," she repeated softly, "with you."

He grabbed her hand, and pulled her to her feet as a rock and roll classic pounded through the speakers.

"Justin, are you sure you want do this? Dance with me?"

"More than anything."

That was a lie. What he wanted to do more than anything was kiss her, but her smile, wide and full of life, captured him. It was the first time he'd seen that smile in almost two weeks. In fact, the last time was when she'd held his son's simple crayon drawing in her hands.

His son.

Dear Reader,

As a writer there is something magical about creating characters, about breathing life into their souls, hearts and minds. Sometimes the people in our books come to us fully formed and overflowing with personality and charm and troubles that only the writer of their stories can fix.

Then there are those in the background, characters who help tell a story, but not their own. They're the sibling, cousin, co-worker, or friend who must have their own dreams, desires and plans for the future, right?

Well, Justin Dillon and Gina Steele were those kinds of people.

His sister fell in love with her brother, but if there were ever two people who never needed to come in contact with each other it was Justin and Gina. But then a chance meeting the day they became co-workers in *The Sheriff's Secret Wife* started a spark that led to a night neither one of them will forget…or talk about. Now that's the beginning of a terrific love story!

Then I met Jacoby and I just knew these three very special people needed my help to find their own happily ever after. I hope you enjoy their story!

Happy reading!

Christyne

DOA

- 8 JAN 2019

1 6 FEB 2019

1 2 SEP 2023

9/18

This book should be returned by the last date stamped above.
You may renew the loan personally, by post or telephone for a
further period if the book is not required by another reader.

www.wakefield.gov.uk

wakefieldcoun
working for

7 0 0 0 0 0 0 0 3 2 4 6 6 0

First published in Great Britain 2012
by Mills & Boon, an imprint of Harlequin (UK) Limited,
Eton House, 18-24 Paradise Road, Richmond, Surrey TW9 1SR

© Christyne Butilier 2011

ISBN: 978 0 263 89436 3
ebook ISBN: 978 1 408 97845 0

923-0512

Harlequin (UK) policy is to use papers that are natural, renewable and recyclable products and made from wood grown in sustainable forests. The logging and manufacturing processes conform to the legal environmental regulations of the country of origin.

Printed and bound in Spain
by Blackprint CPI, Barcelona

Christyne Butler fell in love with romance novels while serving in the United States Navy and started writing her own stories six years ago. She considers selling to Mills & Boon® a dream come true and enjoys writing contemporary romances full of life, love, a hint of laughter and perhaps a dash of danger, too. And there has to be a happily-ever-after or she's just not satisfied.

She lives with her family in central Massachusetts and loves to hear from her readers at chris@christynebutler.com. Or visit her web site at www.christynebutler.com.

Books by Christyne Butler

The Cowboy's Second Chance
The Sheriff's Secret Wife
*A Daddy for Jacoby

*Welcome to Destiny

For Bretton, Christopher, Meaghan, Benjamin,
Kaitlyn and Alyssa
You came into my life unexpectedly and changed
my world forever
I couldn't love you more if you were my very own

To my agent Jennifer Schober for believing in me
and all her hard work

And to Jacoby Ellsbury, leftfielder for my beloved
Boston Red Sox for inspiring the name for my Jacoby

Chapter One

He was scared.

He hated being scared.

Jacoby pulled his ragged teddy bear tighter to his chest and wiped his wet eyes on the soft overalls Clem wore.

That was his bear's name, Clem.

The car swerved and tires squealed. Jacoby shut his eyes tight and buried his face in Clem's fur. He was glad the seat belt worked.

His mama swore and banged her fist against the steering wheel. She cursed the rain, the dark night, their piece of junk car and her miserable life.

Mama did that a lot.

Cursed.

Jacoby didn't like it, especially after a teacher pulled him aside at the start of the school year and told him that nice people didn't talk that way. And he wanted to be nice.

He wished his mama was nicer more.

He wished they were back at Miss Mazie's house, even

if he did have to sleep on the floor in a sleeping bag that scratched his legs. But his mama had packed up their stuff, shoved his clothes into the worn pillowcase he used to carry his books and made him crawl out the window.

He'd turned back and watched her take all the money from a jar Miss Mazie thought they didn't know about. She'd then grabbed two unopened bottles of wine, leaving the almost-empty one where it lay on Miss Mazie's lap.

It was wrong to steal, but Jacoby didn't say anything. The last time he'd told his mama she'd done something wrong, his arm had hurt for three days where she'd grabbed him.

So he'd crept into the backseat next to his pillowcase book bag and kept quiet.

They did this a lot. Moved around.

They'd been with Miss Mazie since New Year's Eve and it would be Easter soon. He'd miss the egg hunt at his school tomorrow and wondered if his teacher would miss him.

He didn't know where they were going, but he hoped they got there soon. Or maybe the rain would stop when the sun came up and he wouldn't be so scared.

Lightning lit up the sky and Jacoby waited for the thunder, but it didn't come. His mama turned back and looked at him, tears on her cheeks.

Now, he was really scared.

She looked silly.

She never looked silly.

Gina Steele studied her reflection in the full-length mirror hanging in the employee break room. She'd been called a lot of *s* words in her life. Scholarly, serious, studious, solemn.

Even scary, thanks to the jerk who'd sat next to her during her freshman year's Introduction to Classic Literature class at the University of Notre Dame. It wasn't her fault at fifteen she'd been the smartest person in the room.

Not to mention the youngest.

Smart was another *s* word associated her. Until today. Today, silly was the only word that fit.

"Oh, I love it!"

Startled, Gina looked into the smiling green eyes that belonged to Barbie Felton, her best friend and fellow waitress, in the mirror's reflection. She focused back on her own face and grimaced. "It's pink."

"It's cool."

"It's bright."

With long blond hair, complete with bangs, and her athletic body, Barbie looked more like Skipper, the iconic doll's little sister, than her namesake. She leaned against the wall. "You can always cover it up. Relax and enjoy it!"

Gina couldn't help but smile as she twirled the inch-wide streak of pink in her hair.

She'd been excited about rekindling her friendship with her elementary school friend when she returned home to Destiny, Wyoming, last winter. Barbie had been one of the few kids who hadn't cared that Gina was years ahead of them in the smarts department.

When Gina had left town after the fifth grade to attend a private school, she and Barbie tried to stay in touch. But like most childhood promises, it hadn't lasted. When Gina started working at The Blue Creek Saloon a few months ago, she was surprised to find that Barbie still lived in town and worked here, too, and they'd reconnected.

"First stop, hair color." Her friend teased, her voice hushed in a dramatic whisper. "Next up…a tattoo!"

"No way!"

Barbie laughed and turned around. Tucking her thumbs into the waistband of her jeans, she tugged the material lower by a few inches. A purple, green and gold dragonfly flitted across her lower back among colorful flowers and green leaves.

A flash of something coursed through Gina. Jealousy?

And was it over the beauty of the artwork or the courage it took to sit still while a needle— "When did you get that?"

"Two weeks ago in Laramie." Barbie grinned over her shoulder.

"And you're just showing it to me now?"

"I wanted to wait until it was completely healed so you'd get the full effect." She spun back around. "It's going to look so cool next week on the beaches of Nassau in my new bikini."

A senior at the University of Wyoming, Barbie was planning a trip to the Bahamas to celebrate spring break. Despite the fact Gina had completed graduate school almost a year ago earning her master's degree, her friend had been after her to join her and her college roommates on the trip.

Gina turned back to the mirror to get a closer look at the streak of hot pink running the length of her dark hair. "I guess this doesn't seem too wild compared to that."

"I noticed you didn't get your hair straightened like you usually do. Hoping to hide the color in all those curls?"

That's exactly what she'd been hoping.

Gina ran her fingers over the rest of her dark brown hair, her glittery, silver nails sparkling in the overhead lights. Another change.

Her own fingernails, always blunt and well-kept, were just fine, but they weren't sexy. Barbie had guaranteed her that tips from customers would improve if Gina took her advice and got the fake extensions. She was right and after a few weeks of getting used to them, Gina found she liked the nails and experimented with new colors every few weeks.

First, her nails. Now, her hair. Was she trying too hard to be like everyone else?

She used to love being different, loved studying and learning, feeding her insatiable appetite for knowledge. But after last summer, all she wanted was to belong, to be one of the girls.

"At least it matches your outfit."

Barbie's remark pulled Gina from her thoughts. She looked down at her light pink T-shirt. "Good thing I passed on the neon green this morning."

"You worried what your mom is going to say?"

"I don't think my mom will even notice. Between the twins, her job and her boyfriend—" Gina shrugged "—she's got a lot on her plate. Anyway, I'm an adult."

Barbie crossed her arms over her chest. "So is it the good sheriff you're worried about?"

"Oh, I'm sure my big brother will have something to say. It might take him a while to notice as he's still playing newly-wed with our boss."

Secretly, Gina was glad Racy Steele, the owner of The Blue Creek Saloon and Gina's new sister-in-law, was keeping Gage so well occupied that he had little time to harass her about her life choices. If he had his way, she'd be putting her degrees and her brains to good use by teaching. But it was high time she stretched her wings and enjoyed herself.

"So what's his name?"

Gina blinked. "Huh?"

"Well, if it's not your family you're rebelling against, it's got to be a guy—ohmigod, is it Justin?"

"No!"

Justin Dillon.

Tall, dark and one-hundred-percent dangerous with his jet-black hair, dark eyes and lean, muscular body. He'd made it clear to Gina the first day they met that he was unavailable and uninterested.

Not that she let that stop her from spending the night with him a few weeks later. That, too, had gone a long way in changing her image from the "smart" girl to—

To what she wasn't sure.

"You're thinking about him."

Gina spun away from the mirror, heading for the boxes

of Blue Creek logo items she'd agreed to put away. "I am not!"

"Hey, I get the attraction." Barbie followed her. "Justin is a total hottie, but he's too old, too obstinate and too—I don't know—"

"Too smart be led around by the nose?"

"Or any other body part," Barbie said, then giggled. "Okay, so I like my men to treat me like the goddess my daddy tells me I am. But you actually scored a visit to Justin's apartment upstairs. That's more than any of the other girls who work here. And you still refuse to spill any details."

"I told you—"

"I know. You forgot your purse after closing that night so you came back inside the bar and found Justin playing pool. Alone," Barbie interrupted, reciting the story Gina had told her. "After a few lessons on the fine art of billiards, one thing led to another and the two of you went upstairs."

"So?" Gina kept her gaze glued to the T-shirts, coffee mugs and key chains she was dividing into separate piles.

"So, inquiring minds want more. When you wouldn't spill, I figured you were over that one night of crazy, un-Gina-like behavior." Barbie leaned against the table and propped her chin on her hands, her stare intent. "Now, I'm not so sure."

Gina's hands stilled as the memory of that night came rushing back to her.

It'd been just the two of them in the bar until three of his old friends had shown up. Justin made it clear they weren't welcome and things got unfriendly fast. The fight lasted only a few minutes and afterward she'd refused to leave, despite his protests. Of course, falling asleep in his bed didn't lend much credibility to her assurance she was staying to keep an eye on him in case he was seriously hurt.

"And I'm guessing you figured no one would've even found out about that night if you hadn't had to step up to be Justin's alibi," Barbie added.

Her friend's comment yanked Gina back to the present. "I wasn't going to let my brother try to pin that fire at Racy's house on Justin. Not when I knew there was no way he was involved."

Once the news of her night with Justin became public, both her mother and older brother had expressed their disappointment over what they assumed had happened that night.

But Gina was tired of being careful. She was also tired of Justin doing his best to ignore her for the last three months.

Much like he'd ignored her that January night when it was just the two of them upstairs in his apartment.

Maybe it was time to do something about that.

They stared at him.

Justin hated it when they stared.

Three months and he was still the talk of the town. Three months since everyone thought the town's ex-con had tarnished the angelic reputation of the sheriff's sister by sleeping with her. Three months and it was still considered hot gossip.

Too bad it never happened.

Justin Dillon ignored the two girls giggling outside the hardware store and shoved another load of wood into the bed of his truck. They were probably in high school and at thirty-two, he was old enough to be their father. Almost.

He slammed the tailgate closed and climbed inside the truck that was older than the teenagers gawking at him, but beggars couldn't be choosers. He started the engine and rolled down the window, letting a spring breeze blow in as he headed down Main Street. April in Wyoming could still bring nasty snowstorms, but lately, it had been sunny and warm.

Good thing, too, as he had plenty of work to do at the cabin. He'd grown tired of living in the makeshift apartment over the bar, especially now that his sister owned the place.

She'd let him stay rent-free, but working in the kitchen and sleeping above it had gotten old.

And the memories from that night with Gina were killing him. Dark hair fanned out over his pillows, lush curves outlined beneath his sheets, soft sighs punctuating her sleep.

Yep, that's all Gina had done.

Sleep.

Him? Not a wink. And it wasn't because of the beating he'd taken that had left him with a pounding headache and sore ribs.

No, it was more like figuring out why Gina, of all people, had stayed with him.

Justin pulled into the lot at The Blue Creek and parked near the back entrance. He wanted to grab the last of his stuff and take it out to the cabin. Thanks to his new brother-in-law purchasing the old campground across the lake from his log home, Justin had somewhere to call his own for the first time in his life.

The good sheriff had agreed to let him stay in one of the two-bedroom cabins in exchange for fixing up the place. Justin figured Gage did it for two reasons. His wife, who also happened to be Justin's sister, had asked him to, and Gage wanted to make sure a repeat performance between his little sister and Justin didn't happen.

Not likely. He was going to make sure of that.

He checked his watch. Almost five. The bar traffic should be light, including the waitstaff, as most of the girls didn't come in until later.

Not that he was trying to avoid anyone.

Stop trying so damn hard to convince yourself.

He heard feminine laughter as he pushed open the door to the employee lounge. Gina stood atop a ladder, reaching to put a box on the top shelf where the items sold out front were stored. Her T-shirt hugged her curves and as she moved, it rose, revealing a few inches of skin at her midsection.

And Ric Murphy, a college kid who worked as one of the bar's bouncers, stood behind her making sure she didn't fall, by conveniently placing one hand on the ladder and the other on the back of one of her jean-clad thighs just beneath her butt.

Justin couldn't hear what the guy was saying, but Gina must have found it funny because she laughed again. The ladder wobbled and Ric put both hands on her instead of steadying the rickety, aged ladder.

Yeah, that made sense.

"Watch out, Ric!" Gina cried, grabbing hold of the metal shelving. "I'm grateful for your help because Barbie had to leave, but if I fall you're going to have to catch me."

"Like that would be a hardship." Ric grinned. "Having a beautiful woman in my arms—"

Justin banged the door against the wall as he entered, heading for the storage locker located to the right of them. "Don't mind me."

Both Gina and Ric jumped and looked at him, but he ignored them. He fumbled with the combination lock, and had to run the combo twice before it sprung open. He yanked open the door and pulled out the boxes he'd stored there.

"Need any help, Dillon?"

Ric's tone was patronizing, but Justin didn't rise to the bait. He kept his back to both of them. For whatever reason, Ric Murphy had made it clear from Justin's first day here that he didn't like him. "I think you've got your hands full."

Gina gasped, but before she could say anything someone in the hall called Ric's name.

"I've got to go. You going to be okay here?" he asked.

"I'll be fine," Gina said. "I'm just about done anyway."

Ric stepped over Justin's stuff and walked out of the room. A long pause filled the air before Gina finally spoke.

Just like Justin figured she would.

"That wasn't very nice."

"That's me," he said, still not looking at her. "Not very nice."

"He was just helping—"

"Sweetheart, if that's all you think he was doing, you've got a lot to learn." He pulled out a couple of sleeping bags and pillows and placed them on the pile.

"What do you care anyway—oh!"

Justin spun. It was a split-second decision. The ladder or the girl. He only had time to grab one and the girl was heading toward him. His hands locked onto Gina's waist, and he pulled her flush against his chest, stopping her fall.

Biting back a curse when the toppling ladder caught him at the knee, he tightened his grip on her waist to keep both of them from tumbling to the floor. Gina twisted in his arms and he found his nose inches from being buried in her soft curves.

"Dammit, hold still." He expelled his comment with a hiss.

She froze, but her body responded, easily visible through her cotton T-shirt.

He could have set her to the floor, but instead he slowly dragged her down the length of him, causing that soft T-shirt to ride up even more, until they were eye to eye.

"Did you do that on purpose?" he asked, surprised at the huskiness of his voice.

"Do what?"

He didn't know if she was blushing because of the closeness of their bodies or the fact her soft words matched his. "Reach too far so I'd catch you when you fell."

The pink tinges of her skin darkened. "Are you crazy? Put me down." She squirmed and pushed against his shoulders.

"You are down."

"I can't feel the floor beneath my feet."

"Yeah, I've been told I have that effect on women."

Her blue eyes widened, that famous Steele blue color

everyone in her family shared, and her lips parted. A musky, exotic scent lifted from her skin. He pulled in a deep breath, instantly associating it with the spicy-yet-sweet flavor of cinnamon with just a hint of sugar added for flavoring.

It brought to mind the rack of spices he used in the kitchen on a daily basis. On more than one occasion he'd grabbed the tin of dusky, reddish-brown powder whether or not cinnamon was called for in the recipe.

Damn, this girl was trouble with a capital *T*. She was also innocent with a capital *I*.

Gina was twenty-two years old, ten years his junior. Justin had learned enough about her in the last three months to know she was one part intelligence, one part wholesome and completely out of his league.

"Justin…"

Her voice, low, throaty and way too enticing, snapped him back to reality. He quickly set her away from him, desperate to escape the effect she was having on him, both physically and mentally.

It was then he saw the pink in her hair. It looked like she'd tried to hide it, tucked back behind one ear, but her fall had caused the bright streak of color to spring forward and rest against her cheek.

He knew it was wrong, he even commanded his hand not to move, but his fingers had a mind of their own. They reached up and with the slightest movement, the curl wrapped around his calloused finger.

"What's this? Your nonconformist side coming out?"

She jerked her head to the side, but he held tight with gentle pressure. "Hmm, wonder what big brother is going to say?"

"Gage doesn't care what I do to my hair." The words were strong, but there was little confidence in her voice. "Are you going to let go of me?"

He didn't want to. What he wanted was to wrap his finger

completely around the strand of hair until his hand curled around the back of her neck. Then he'd run his thumb along her jaw, tilt her head upward as his mouth came down—

Whoa, back up! You've vowed to stay away from this girl, remember?

Justin released her and turned away. He grabbed two boxes and headed for the doorway when Ric appeared in it.

"Hey, Dillon. You're wanted out front."

"What for? I'm not working tonight."

"You've got a visitor." Ric looked at the ladder lying on the floor. "Hey, someone said they thought they heard a noise— what happened? Gina, you all right?"

Justin put down the boxes and walked out of the room, Gina's breathless assurance she was okay ringing in his ears.

Was he stupid?

Gina was smart. Too smart. Did she know he'd been inches away from kissing her? He hadn't looked into her eyes, hadn't read her body language. Pink lips and a pink curl was all he'd focused on, but she must've known…

Just like she had to know he'd been inches away from kissing her three months ago.

He'd been teaching her how to shoot pool for almost an hour and she'd finally gotten the right ball into the right pocket. She'd jumped into his arms and hugged him and he'd never been more tempted in his life.

Then they'd been rudely, but thankfully, interrupted.

Pushing the memory from his head, he entered the main area of The Blue Creek Saloon and saw the tables and booths starting to fill up with the Friday night regulars for dinner. Some would stay for the live music and dancing later and the spring night would bring out the college crowd once the sun went down.

He spotted Jackie, the assistant manager, near the kitchen entrance and headed her way.

A tall blonde and little boy standing nearby hit his radar, but only because he made sure to always be aware of who was in his personal space. A habit he'd picked up in prison, which is why it still bothered him those punks had gotten the jump on him and Gina that night.

"Murphy said I had a visitor?" he asked when Jackie turned to him.

"Yes, you do. This young lady—"

"Justin! Finally!"

The blonde launched herself into his arms and Justin had no choice but to catch her. Unlike Gina's curves, however, this girl was skin and bones. Her hair and clothes were dirty and she smelled like she hadn't bathed in a while.

After catching his balance, Justin peeled her arms from around his neck just as Gina and Ric walked in from the back hall. "Ah, I'm sorry, but I don't know—"

"It's me, Zoe! Zoe Ellis?" The girl clutched his hands. "You must remember me."

He didn't. Over the last three months, his encounters with the opposite sex consisted mostly of conversations with his sister Racy, and his coworkers. Yeah, there had been that girl he'd celebrated his release with when he first got out, but this wasn't her. And he'd gotten more than a few offers for company from a couple of the waitresses, especially after everyone thought he and Gina had slept together—

Nope, not going there.

Justin forced his attention back on the girl, realizing he'd missed most of what she'd said.

"—and then we got a hotel room and didn't come out for three days. I tell ya, I can still remember how you—"

"Look, you must have me mistaken with someone else. I've been…gone for quite a few years and only got back in town about three months ago."

"Well, I know it's been a while, eight years in fact, but I never forgot." The girl reached for the little boy next to her.

Justin took in the child's dark hair and eyes, seeing both fear and curiosity in his gaze as he clung to a scruffy-looking teddy bear and a dirty pillowcase that bulged at odd angles.

"In fact, I've had a constant reminder of those crazy few days," she continued. "Meet Jacoby. Your son."

Chapter Two

Justin couldn't move. He wanted to. His legs screamed at him to run. Run hard and run fast and never look back. Ashamed at that thought, he shoved it aside to concentrate on what the girl had just said.

"My what?"

She yanked on the kid's T-shirt, forcing him to stumble forward. "Your son. Jacoby Joseph Ellis."

At the mention of his father's name as this child's middle name, Justin's gaze snapped from the boy, whose downcast eyes were centered on his own dirty sneakers, one sporting a big hole in the toe, back to her.

"How— He can't— He can't be more than five years old. I've been in pri—" He paused and pulled in a deep breath. "I've been out of touch for the last seven years."

"He's small for his age. His seventh birthday was in January. If you count back nine months…"

April. Eight-plus years ago. A few months before he and Billy Joe had been busted for drug trafficking.

A bust he'd actually helped with.

Tired of the life he'd been living, Justin had anonymously slipped insider information to the cops on the drug ring he and his brother worked for. The guilt and fear over what he'd been doing had caused him to live in an alcohol-induced haze for weeks. No drugs, though. He'd never touched the stuff, despite his chosen profession, but partying had included a wild weekend he and his buddies had spent in a small town in Colorado.

Was it possible he *was* this boy's father?

He tried to remember the girl as she rummaged in the large purse at her shoulder. She pulled out a wrinkled piece of paper. "Here's his birth certificate."

Justin read his name listed as the boy's father. "If this is true, why now? Why not get in touch with me when he was born?"

"What could you have done from where you were?"

"You knew where I was?" He clenched the certificate in his fist. "But you never thought to tell me you had my baby?"

"Ah, it might be better if you all move to one of the back booths?"

Justin looked up to find Gina standing behind the little boy. He read curiosity, concern and another emotion he couldn't identify in her eyes. She looked from him to the main area of the bar. He then noticed both Jackie and Ric had disappeared, but the tables had filled up, and most were watching them.

Damn, he should've thought of that. "Yeah, that's a good idea."

He marched to the other side of the bar and slid into the end booth. He watched Zoe eagerly follow, not even looking back to make sure the boy was with her. She plopped down next to Justin, moving in much too close.

"How about burgers and fries for you two?" Gina asked as she helped the little boy get settled into the opposite seat.

"And sodas," Zoe added.

"Maybe milk for your son?"

Justin picked up on the edge in Gina's voice as she stared at him. What? She expected him to make that call?

Zoe waved away the question, her attention on Justin as she rested her hand on his arm. "Oh, he drinks soda all the time."

"Except at school. I have chocolate milk there."

Justin shook off Zoe's touch as the boy spoke for the first time, even though it seemed like he was talking to his bear instead of to one of the adults.

"Chocolate milk is my favorite. I'll be right back." Gina's smile for the boy was sweet, but it disappeared as she shot Justin a hard look before walking away.

"Is she your girlfriend?" Zoe asked.

"What? No, she's…a coworker." Justin smoothed out the birth certificate and folded it in half. "I work here at The Blue Creek. How did you know where to find me?"

"I figured this was the best place to start. You talked about this bar that weekend we spent together. Besides, who can forget a town called Destiny?"

The pieces were starting to fall back into place. He and his buddies had gone on a road trip. They'd ended up at a house party and a couple of guys had been in the kitchen giving a girl a hard time. He'd stepped in and she'd stuck by his side the rest of the night.

And the rest of the weekend.

"You told me your name was Susie," he said, more details surfacing in his foggy brain.

"Yeah, I lied." She shrugged. "It was just for fun."

"How do I know you're not lying now? Just because you put my name on that piece of paper—"

Gina appeared with two plates of food and the drinks, cutting off his words. She must've taken someone else's order to get back so fast. After everything was on the table, she turned to the boy. "Would you like to wash your hands before you eat?"

Justin thought the kid needed to be scrubbed from head to toe, but he kept quiet. Zoe dug into the food, ignoring everything else.

"Okay," the boy said.

Gina held out her hand and he went with her. "I'll take him to the kitchen."

His mother didn't reply, so Justin nodded. Waiting until they were out of earshot, he grabbed for the soda the same moment Zoe did.

"Hey!"

"You let your son go off with a total stranger?"

Zoe looked at him. "Like she's going to run off with the kid? She looks like she's barely out of college."

If he remembered correctly, Zoe was a few years older than Gina. Unless that had been a lie, too. "You told me you were nineteen back then. Was that the truth?"

She tucked the birth certificate into the pocket of his T-shirt. "Yes. Now, can I have my drink?"

He handed over the soda. "You still haven't told me why you never got a hold of me."

"I thought about it when I found out I was pregnant, but then I heard about your arrest. Like I said, there was nothing you could do from where you were heading and heck, we were just a one-night—one-weekend stand." She paused to take a long swallow from the cup. "I figured I could handle things myself."

"So, why look me up now?"

"I read you got out of prison early for good behavior. Hey, I'm not going to lie, the last seven years have been hard. I'm not too proud to come and ask for help."

He didn't know what to say. Was the kid his? Without a DNA test, he couldn't be sure, no matter how the dates matched up.

Gina returned with the boy, who started in on his food with an enthusiasm that left Justin wondering when was the last time they'd eaten a meal.

"You make sure you eat all that," she directed her comments to her son. "I'm gonna go to the bathroom. You be good and don't give your dad any trouble, you hear?"

The ketchup bottle in the boy's hand stilled at he looked at his mom with dark eyes. They shifted to lock on to Justin before the child nodded solemnly.

Justin sat mute, having no idea how to respond to her words. He watched her slip out of the booth and head for the front foyer where the restrooms were located. When she disappeared through the swinging doors, he turned his attention back to the boy, noticing they had the same dark hair and eyes.

Jacoby Ellis. His son?

If it was true, shouldn't he feel something? A pull? A spark? That unexplained connection between parent and child?

He doubted his father ever had felt that toward him, his brother or sister. Joseph Dillon hadn't had a paternal bone in his body. Justin had only been five when their mother died, but there was never any doubt that she'd loved all her children with a fierce devotion. He was still able to recall the warmth of her touch. And the sound of her tears.

He shook off the memory and noticed the fries were going into the boy's mouth faster than he could chew. "Hey, take it easy. No one's going to take away your plate until you're finished, okay?"

Those dark eyes looked at him again. The boy didn't speak, but he did slow down. Justin watched him eat for a few minutes, then his own stomach rumbled and he found himself wishing Gina had brought him a burger, too.

Like magic, a plate with a Blue Creek Super Burger appeared in front of him.

Gina stood at the table, her arms crossed. "I figured watching them eat was making you hungry. Besides, something tells me you're going to need to keep up your strength."

Justin scowled at her, but grabbed the burger anyway.

"Does that taste good?" She turned her attention to the kid and he nodded, too busy sucking chocolate milk through a straw to reply.

"Where's your friend?" Her voice was low as she directed the question back at Justin.

He forced down a mouthful of food. "Ladies' room. Can you believe this? Damn, what a freaking mess—"

"Justin!" Gina cut him off, dropping her hands to the table. She leaned forward, cutting off his view of the boy. Not that he was looking at the kid with Gina's curves practically laid out in front of him.

Geez, now was not the time for his mind to take *that* detour. "What?"

"Watch your language."

Her words came out in a whisper so low that he had to read her lips to get what she was saying. "What did I say?"

She straightened and took a step back, again with the crossed arms. A toss of her head sent her curls—including that darn pink one—flying over her shoulder.

"It's what you were going to say. You've got little ears here," she whispered. "You need to be careful."

Justin sighed. She was right. Something told him it was a position Gina Steele, egghead extraordinaire, was probably very used to.

"Okay, I get it. Can you do me a favor and check on Zoe?" he asked. "She's a little…upset."

Gina stared at him for a long moment, then nodded and left.

"Your mom will be right back," Justin said.

The boy only stared at him and clutched his bear tighter. Justin grabbed his burger and nodded to the boy's half-eaten food. The kid started munching again, but the bear stayed right on his lap.

A few minutes later, Gina came back to the table. Alone.

"What's going—" Justin read confusion on her face. "Where's Zoe?"

"The ladies' room was empty." Gina again kept her voice low as she turned away from the boy. "I checked with Ric, he's working the front door. He didn't see her leave. I even checked the parking lot. Nothing."

A sucker punch hit Justin square in the gut, harder than the one delivered less than a half hour earlier when Zoe had walked back into his life.

She left? She walked away from her own son?

He stared at the boy, who kept his eyes glued to his plate.

"I think we should call Gage."

The mention of Gina's brother—now his brother-in-law—caused a familiar ripple of unease. At best, he and the sheriff tolerated each other. Usually from a distance.

"We need to search the place." Justin slid to the end of the booth. "Maybe she just wanted to find a quiet spot to…I don't know, to think, to pull herself together."

"Ric and a few others are looking for her." Gina put a hand on his shoulder, stopping him. "I'll call my brother…just in case. You need to stay here."

Justin nodded.

Gina left again. He eyed the food, but his appetite was gone. His wasn't the only one. The boy had stopped eating, his gaze glued to the table. Justin knew he should say something, but his mind was a blank.

Less than fifteen minutes later, Gina was back with her brother right on her heels, but she disappeared when Gage started talking.

"So, what's going on?" Gage said. "Who's the little guy?"

The boy shrank into the corner of the booth, his eyes locked on the newcomer. Despite being the sheriff of Destiny for the last decade, Gage rarely wore a uniform. Fully recovered from a gunshot wound that had him in the hospital a few months ago and at just over six feet tall, he could be pretty imposing even in jeans, his trademark leather jacket and Stetson.

Justin rose from the booth. His height matched his brother-in-law's and blocked the boy's view. "His name is Jacoby Ellis," he said, keeping his voice low. "And I'm told—not that I'm a hundred-percent sure—he's my son."

The widening of Gage's eyes and the bracketing of his hands on his hips were his only reaction to the news.

Justin fought against mimicking Gage's body posture and kept his hands loose at his side. "His mother showed up, introduced us and grabbed a bite to eat. The last I knew she was headed to the bathroom."

"How long ago was that?"

"Twenty minutes. Maybe a little bit more."

Gage nodded. "The mother's name?"

"Zoe Ellis."

Gina reappeared at her brother's shoulder. "Racy's here. She suggested we go to her office. It's more private and this place is filling up with customers."

Justin nodded and turned around, but Gina was already there. She grabbed Jacoby's pillowcase and got him out of the booth. Justin and Gage followed. Racy's golden retriever greeted them when they opened the office door.

"Oh, it's okay." Gina squatted next to the boy when he shrank back, bumping into Justin's legs. "This is Jack and he's the sweetest pup. Here, let him smell your hand."

Jacoby stretched out his fingers. Jack proceeded to sniff

them, then immediately moved in to offer a few quick licks to the boy's face.

Justin reached for the dog's collar, but stopped when the sound of the child's laughter filled the air.

Followed by a gasp from Justin's sister.

He looked up to see Racy's gaze flying between him and Jacoby. "Sis, what's wrong?"

Racy turned toward her desk and rummaged in one of the drawers. Justin and Gage went to her, while Gina settled the boy and the dog on the leather couch against the far wall.

"Honey, what are you looking for?" Gage asked.

Racy pulled out a manila envelope from the last drawer. "This," she said, dumping the contents on her desk.

Photographs, black-and-white and colored, likely decades old, scalloped edges on some and rounded corners on others. She flipped through the images until she pulled out a small one.

"Thank goodness I had these stored here instead of at the house. They would've been lost in the fire. Here's your proof."

"Proof?" Justin asked.

"Gina told me about your surprise visitor and that precious little boy." Her gaze lingered on the occupants on the couch. "As soon as you all walked in the door, I knew."

"Knew what?"

"Look at this picture." She shoved the photograph into his hands. "That's you. First grade."

It was him. But it was also Jacoby. The image could've been of the same person. The dark hair and eyes, the square line of the jaw even at such a young age. They even wore the same colored T-shirt, red.

"Maybe you better fill us in completely," Gage said, taking out a small notebook. "If his mother has taken off, we'll need everything you know to try and find her."

"I think I'll head out now."

Justin turned to see Gina at the door. The boy was reading a book he must've pulled from his pillowcase. One hand turned the pages; the other was busy scratching the neck of a very content Jack.

"No, stay."

Gina's elegant brows rose at his tone.

"Please," Justin quickly added. "The kid seems—he seems at ease with you."

Her fingers tightened on the doorknob and Justin thought she was going to leave anyway. But she gave him a quick nod and moved back to the couch.

Justin turned back to the sheriff and his sister. They both stared at him. He ignored the unspoken questions in their gazes and told them what had happened in the last hour. Then he described how he had met Zoe eight years ago.

"I didn't believe her at first. Maybe I didn't want to. Hell... me? A father?" Justin winced and waved the photograph in the air. "But seeing this..."

"Okay, let's see if the boy can help us out," Gage said.

He couldn't. Or wouldn't.

After answering a few questions that revealed the name of his elementary school, a town in Colorado and that his mom's car was tan and a piece of junk, Jacoby clammed up, refusing to answer any more.

"It's not much, but I'll start with finding out exactly where Templeton, Colorado, is." Gage rose from where he'd knelt by the couch. He motioned for Justin and Racy to join him back at Racy's desk. "I'm heading to the office to make an official report. Now, what are we going to do with this little guy tonight? Or the next couple of nights? It'll probably take until Monday or Tuesday before we get anywhere."

"Why can't he stay with Justin?" Gina asked from across the room.

Justin turned, her question yet another sucker punch to his

gut. At this rate, his insides would be black and blue. "Are you serious?"

"You are his father."

"We don't know that—"

Both Gage and Justin spoke at the same time.

"—officially," Gage finished. When Gina opened her mouth to protest, he held up his hand to cut her off. "Yes, I agree all the signs point in that direction, but until a test can be done we don't know for sure. I can place a call to child services. They can find a local foster home."

The sheriff's words caused the pain sitting square in Justin's gut to radiate throughout his body.

The entire room faded as the memory of his father yelling, words slurred thanks to the alcohol running through his veins, took over. He'd often threaten him, Billy Joe and Racy with horror stories of being shipped off to child services. At the time, the unknown hell he'd described sounded a lot worse than the hell they were living.

"Justin?"

Racy's voice pulled him from the memory, in time to see the door close behind Gina. She must think he was actually going to—

He turned back to his sister and Gage when he felt a small hand, clammy and cold, against his own. He looked down. Jacoby stood next to him, squeezing his fingers, and those dark eyes stared up at him.

"He's coming home with me," Justin said.

The boy didn't speak or smile, but the haunted look that filled his eyes when they had tried to get information about his mother from him faded.

"You sure?" Gage asked. "What kind of condition is the cabin in?"

"It's a mess but livable. I've been staying there for the last couple of weeks."

"Having a little boy around is totally different from being

there alone," Racy added. "Do you have enough food? What about heat? It still gets pretty chilly at night. We've got room at our place—"

"We'll be fine," Justin insisted. "The fireplace is working. And I can't believe you're really asking me—the best cook you've got—if I've got enough food."

Racy smiled at that. "Okay, you've got me there. Gage told me you got those antique kitchen appliances working again, but—"

"No *buts*." He hoped the confidence in his voice sounded real, because the words rang hollow as they rolled off his tongue. "We'll be fine."

An hour later, he wasn't so sure.

He'd finished loading his truck with Gage's help, then he and Jacoby headed out. Seeing his place through the eyes of a child who stood in the doorway clutching his meager belongings made him realize the cabin was more a construction zone-slash-bachelor pad than a home.

It had grown dark on the ride out to the lake and the only lights in the cabin were in the kitchen, the bath and one secondhand lamp sitting on the floor in the living room. He'd turned on the lamp, and a fire helped warm up the place, both in temperature and looks.

He didn't say much to Jacoby except to repeatedly warn him away from the tools and construction materials that seemed to fascinate the boy. Of course, the kid hadn't said two words since he'd hugged Racy's dog goodbye at The Blue Creek.

"I've got to get some stuff out of the truck." Justin stood near the open door, the dark night an alluring draw. "Just sit there until I'm done and don't touch anything, okay?"

Jacoby looked at the folding chair that sat inches off the floor. He dropped into it, pulling his pillowcase to his feet and tucking his bear into his lap. The bag, torn and dirty, was definitely on its last leg.

Justin could relate.

What in the hell was he doing? He didn't have any experience with kids other than being one himself. Agreeing to bring Jacoby home had been instinct, born out of his hellish childhood memories. He was flying blind here, praying he was doing the right thing.

Whatever that might be.

He stepped outside, leaving the oak-planked door open, glad for the screen door he'd installed just yesterday. The overhead lamp automatically came on, lighting up the porch that ran the length of the cabin. The night air had a bracing chill, and he inhaled deeply as he stepped onto the dirt driveway. There was still a load of wood to get out of the back of the truck, but at the moment, he just gazed up at the stars.

This morning, his biggest worry was deciding which of the bedrooms in the cabin to tackle next. This afternoon, it had been reaffirming his vow to stay far away from Gina, knowing he was the wrong guy for her despite how great it felt to have her in his arms again.

And now? Now he might be a father.

A crashing noise had Justin racing back inside. Jacoby stood at the kitchen sink, an overturned wooden crate next to him and a plastic cup on the floor.

"I was thirsty," he said.

Surprised that the boy had finally spoken, Justin pulled in a deep breath and commanded his heart to stop its wild pounding in his chest. It wasn't listening.

He grabbed a water bottle from the refrigerator and plopped down on the overturned crate. "Here."

The boy didn't move.

"It's okay. You can have it."

"I won't finish all that."

Justin unscrewed the lid and offered it again. "No worries. We can put the top back on."

The boy took the bottle and drank. It was then Justin noticed the photograph clutched in his hand. "What's that?"

His small fist, and the photo, disappeared behind his back.

"I'm not going to take it. I'm just wondering who's…" Justin's voice faded.

Could that image be a clue to finding Zoe? He reached into his T-shirt pocket and pulled out the photograph he'd tucked there, behind Jacoby's birth certificate. He showed it to the boy. "See this?"

Curiosity had the boy leaning forward. "It's me."

Justin's gut tightened, a reflex against the emotional punches he'd been taking all night. "No, actually that's me. Back when I was your age."

Jacoby slowly pulled the picture out and turned it around. "This is you, too."

Creased down the middle, the fold split the image of a couple sitting arm in arm on a beat-up sofa. They held beers in their hands and goofy smiles on their faces. Him and Zoe. It must've been taken the night they met.

And the hits kept coming.

Justin swallowed hard before he spoke. "Did your mom give you that?"

The boy nodded. "She said it's her and my daddy. She said my daddy had gone away for a long time, but soon I'd go and live with him and he'd take care of me 'cause she can't anymore."

There it was.

The final blow. A solid right hook that sent him to the mat. Thank goodness he was already sitting because he doubted his knees would've held him upright.

She'd planned this.

Zoe had come to town purposely to leave her son with him.

That meant even if by some strange twist, he wasn't the kid's father, he was still left holding the bag. One that was every bit as precious as the one Jacoby dragged along behind him.

Chapter Three

"I don't know about this. It might not be a good idea."

Gina looked at Jack. The golden retriever sat on his haunches in the passenger seat, tongue lolling out the side of his mouth, panting in anticipation.

"I've been overflowing with less-than-stellar ideas lately. Just look at my hair. Do you think I'm doing the right thing?"

Jack barked once and she took it as an affirmative.

Her car crawled over the dirt road, the beam from the headlights bouncing off the thick forest of trees. She glanced at the clock. Almost eight. She still had over an hour before she was supposed to meet Barbie and her friends in Laramie.

"Then again, I'm sure everything we're bringing is needed." She glanced at the list resting in the cup holder. "Yes, this is a good idea, a great idea. I can do this. I'll just drop the stuff off, make sure they're okay and leave. How's that sound?"

Jack leaned forward and licked her ear. Another yes.

She pulled up next to Justin's battered pickup and cut the engine. She hadn't been out here since last fall when Gage had shown the family around his newly purchased land. Her older brother had wanted this old camp ever since he'd bought the ten acres on the other side of the lake where he'd built the log home he and Racy now lived in.

With the help of the full moon and clear skies, she could make out a few of the eight cabins that dotted the shore on this side of the lake, one of the largest right in front of her.

Justin's cabin.

She waited, but when no one stepped outside, she shoved the list into her pocket, grabbed the laundry basket from the backseat and headed for the front porch. Jack led the way.

The smell of freshly cut wood mixed with the pungent scent from the pine trees that surrounded the house. A light shone on newly built porch planks that stretched the length of the cabin.

Even as her breath puffed before her face in chilled air, she could easily picture a pillow-laden swing hanging from overhead chains at the far end of the porch, facing the water. A perfect spot to enjoy a cool glass of lemonade on a hot summer evening while listening to the lake and the woods...

"Oh, stop daydreaming," she muttered and turned back, giving the screen door a quick knock while managing to hold on to the heavy basket.

Nothing.

She leaned closer and peered inside through the mesh. There, in the kitchen. Justin sat on a crate with his back to her while the little boy, barely visible beyond Justin's wide shoulders, stood directly in front of him.

Should she interrupt? Maybe she should leave the basket—

No. She'd decided it was important enough to pull these things together and get them here. Tonight. Add the touch of guilt she'd felt because she'd actually thought Justin was going to let that sweet little boy go off with strangers…

Okay, deep breath.

She knocked harder and this time Jack added a deep woof.

Justin spun around, his dark piercing eyes fixed on her. A ripple moved across her lower stomach, momentarily taking her breath away. It was a familiar visceral response to this man she still hadn't gotten used to. It'd happened the first time she'd ever laid eyes on him, that afternoon in Racy's office back in January, and every time he'd looked at her since.

Because he didn't just look at her. No, his gaze locked with hers, like a radar beam on a target. And she was always the one who looked away first.

Except for the night he'd been battered and hurt. That night it'd been Justin who couldn't hold her gaze as he sat on the opposite side of the room while she crawled beneath his sheets—

She scrubbed the memory from her mind, but noted that same intuitive feeling had taken root low in her belly earlier today when he'd held her in his arms in the storeroom. She hadn't fallen on purpose, no matter what he thought. And once she was in his arms, her femme fatale plan to get him to pay attention to her had gone up in smoke the moment his dark eyes latched on to her.

Why was it she could use her newly acquired flirting skills on Ric with no problems? Because he flirted back? Not Justin.

He didn't flirt.

He smoldered.

Gina pasted a smile on her face, and decided to forgo the flirting and settled for friendly. "Hi, am I interrupting?"

That was stupid. Of course, she was interrupting.

The boy leaned around Justin. "Jack!"

The dog barked in response, and Gina angled one leg to keep the animal from jumping against the screen. "Hope you don't mind us stopping by. When I heard about— When I found out you…"

Her voice trailed off as Justin gave a deep sigh, rose and headed for the door.

He didn't want her here. And if a little boy hadn't been standing in the middle of the room waiting to see Jack, he probably would've slammed the inside door in her face.

Instead he put his hand against the frame and paused, but then pushed open the screen door. Jack crossed the threshold and headed straight for the boy, but Gina waited to be invited.

"I'm not really in the mood for company."

She turned her gaze up at him. Way up. She stood only five and a half feet tall, even in her favorite Tony Lama boots, and Justin easily towered over her. "I've got plans. I won't be here long."

Silence stretched between them. He filled the doorway with his broad shoulders, his hands braced on the frame and the mussed tufts of his dark hair skimming the top of the doorway.

He pushed the door open wide. "Well?"

She didn't move forward, but she didn't back away either. It was a small victory. "Well what?"

He cocked his head to one side, his gaze burning a path from her face to her boots as he took his leisurely time studying her. "Are you going to stand out there like Little Red Riding Hood with her basket," he asked, "or are you coming in?"

She swallowed hard and glanced down. Beneath her jean jacket, her long-sleeve jersey top was a deep wine color and the lace-edged tank top that peeked from beneath the scooped neckline was black, but she guessed it was close enough.

"Coming in."

She hefted the basket and took a step, bumping it into Justin's midsection when he didn't move back fast enough.

"I'll take that."

He let go of the door and reached for the basket's handles. The heat of his calloused hands scorched her skin, taking her back again to when he'd caught her midtumble from the ladder. It was the closest they'd been in each other's personal space in months.

Even when they happened to be working the same shifts at the bar, they'd managed to keep a respectable distance from each other, especially after he'd made it clear he wasn't interested in being friends, or anything else.

Not after that cold January night when he'd laughed at her attempts at playing pool and then demonstrated, his strong arms wrapped around her, how to hold a pool cue. He'd taught her to aim, shoot and celebrated with her when she'd finally managed to get the ball into the pocket. A celebration that she was sure was going to include his mouth on hers until—

With a mental shake, she dispelled the memory, pulled her hands from the basket and scooted into the cabin. An oversize toolbox and a variety of power tools littered the floor. The only furniture was a couple of camping chairs. Rolled sleeping bags sat atop a group of rumpled blankets.

Cardboard boxes, some open, others still taped up, lined one wall of the large room. Nothing covered the many windows, allowing the dark night to creep in. The only bright spot was a cheery fire blazing in a beautiful stone fireplace.

"Hey, Jacoby."

He sat on the floor, teddy bear on his lap and a water bottle in one hand. Jack laid next to him, flat on his back, never one to pass up a belly rub. "Watch out, that mangy mutt will expect you to rub him for hours."

Jacoby offered a small grin, but his gaze shifted past her. He then ducked his head and concentrated on the dog.

"What are you doing here?" Justin crossed the room and

placed the laundry basket on the countertop that separated the kitchen from the living room. "Does my sister know Jack's with you?"

She followed, her gaze drawn to the darkened kitchen. The antique stove and refrigerator, complete with chrome accents, reminded her of her late grandmother's house.

A throat clearing told her he was waiting for an answer.

"Of course Racy knows." She joined him at the counter. "She's the one who suggested I bring him after seeing Jacoby with him earlier."

"So your brother knows you're here, too?"

"Not that it matters, but my brother is at work. I went back to the bar because I forgot my paycheck…" she paused, then lowered her voice "…with all the craziness earlier. Racy told me about you bringing Jacoby home instead of—well, you know—"

"Passing the kid off to yet another stranger?" Justin half turned, resting his arms on the basket. His tone matched hers. "Throwing another curveball at him? I mean, it's not like he's had enough to deal with today."

Okay, she deserved that. She tucked a strand of curls behind one ear that included the pink one and forced herself to look him in the eye. "That was so unfair of me. I apologize."

The uncertainty in his gaze was achingly familiar; she'd seen the same wariness in another set of dark brown eyes.

Jacoby's.

"I figured you might not have stuff a little boy needs." She pulled a paper bag from the basket and set it on the counter. "I grabbed a half-gallon of milk, some apples and bananas, a box of cereal that my brother Garrett refused to touch. Too healthy, he says—"

"I've been living here for the last few weeks," Justin interrupted her. "I do have the means to keep from starving."

"Oh, well…I didn't think you'd have real food."

He waved a hand toward the refrigerator. "What do you think that is? An oversize beer cooler?"

"I meant food for a child."

He crossed his arms over his chest. "And what kind of food do they eat exactly?"

Gina opened her mouth, but clamped it shut again when she realized she didn't have an answer.

"The appliances might be ancient, but despite their outward appearance, they're clean and in working order." He took a step back. "Go ahead, take a look."

He should be angry that she'd assumed he lived in a place equivalent to a fraternity house with nothing but beer and junk food, but he wasn't. He sounded almost amused.

Gina's cheeks flamed with embarrassment that probably matched the pink in her hair. She grabbed the bag and made a wide circle around him into the kitchen. She pulled on the refrigerator's tarnished handle and the door popped open. Light spilled out, highlighting the aged but spotlessly clean interior and its contents. Milk, orange juice, bottled water, eggs and sandwich meats lined the three shelves. Two drawers at the bottom were filled with fruits and vegetables. A half-dozen beer bottles stood in line on the narrow door shelf. It took only a moment to put most of her meager offerings inside.

"I brought a pack of baloney, but the meat drawer is full." She didn't look at him, only tapped a fingernail against the metal door to the inside freezer. "Can I put it in here?"

"Sure."

She opened the door and shoved it inside, noting the frozen chicken and steaks, a few ready-to-eat pizzas and the open end of a bright yellow box. She looked over her shoulder. "You even have popsicles...."

Her voice faded as he moved into the darkened kitchen, stopping to lean against the counter. The only light in the room came from the open refrigerator, but considering Justin's height, it only shined on his lower half, emphasizing long legs encased in well-worn jeans.

"I like the taste of something sweet every now and then," he said.

Don't ask, don't ask, don't ask.

It took pushing her tongue against the roof of her mouth to stop from wondering aloud what his favorite flavor was. It worked, just barely, and she closed the door. She offered a silent prayer the dimness of the room was enough to hide the blush heating her face.

A snap sounded and the room flooded with light from twin pendent fixtures that hung from the ceiling directly over a center butcher-block island.

She couldn't resist looking around, noting that despite the chipped countertops, cabinets sporting faded white paint, some missing their doors entirely, the room was clean and well stocked. A toaster sat on the counter near a dish drainer and a trio of new windows, filled the wall over the sink.

"What were you expecting? A heap of fast-food containers and empty beer bottles?"

It was as if he could read her mind.

Shame filled her. Three steps and she invaded his personal space, laying her hand on his folded arms. "Justin, I'm sorry I misjudged you. I should've known the first room you'd have fixed up and in working order would've been the kitchen. You're a chef, after all."

He straightened and stepped away from her touch. "I'm not a chef. I'm a cook. Plain and simple."

He was hardly that. The staff had raved over the dishes he'd invented and Racy was smart enough to add many of them to The Blue Creek's menu. It still amazed Gina he'd learned that skill in prison.

"I hafta go the bathroom."

Both of them swung around when the small voice came from the living room.

"Okay," Justin said. "Go."

Jacoby just stood there, his bear in one hand and the other resting on Jack's neck as the dog sat next to him.

A pained expression came over Justin's features, but when he caught her looking at him, he quickly erased it. "You don't have to ask for permission. You can just go. It's right through that doorway. The light is on the outside."

Jacoby headed across the room, the dog on his heels.

"Jack, stay. He doesn't need your help—" Gina said.

Both stopped, but only Jack looked at them, the corners of his mouth curving upward into the humanlike grin that always seemed to be on the dog's face.

"I don't care if he comes with me."

Gina looked at Justin, who only shrugged.

"Then I guess it's okay," she said to the boy, "but be careful, he's known to drink out of the toilet."

Jacoby turned, his face screwed up with disgust. "Eww, gross."

Gina grinned. "Totally gross."

The boy and dog disappeared through the doorway and the sound of a door closing echoed through the cabin.

Justin moved back to the counter. "Remind me never to let that dog kiss me again. So, what else do you have in here?"

"Ah, sheets and a blanket, which I can now see you don't need." She waved at the bedding on the floor near the fireplace as Justin dug into the basket. "A few books, a night-light—"

"What is this?"

Gina gasped.

Swinging from Justin's index finger was her new black satin bra, complete with lace and a skull-and-crossbones pattern mixed with the word *vixen* in bold letters over each cup.

"I'm guessing this isn't for me?"

"Give me that!"

Gina grabbed for the bra, but Justin easily held it out of her reach as he stepped backward into the living room.

"So where are the matching panties?" he asked.

On her. She'd meant to wear the set, but she hadn't been able to find the matching bra. Now she knew why. Not that she'd tell him that. Then she realized she didn't have to, her silence gave him his answer. A hot and intense spark flashed in his gaze. No, that couldn't be right. It had to be the flames from the nearby fire reflecting off those dark eyes, because seconds later it was gone.

A loud creaking preceded the opening of the bathroom door. Justin turned toward it. She grabbed for the bra, but he closed his grip. A quick tug-of-war ensued before she won and stuffed the sexy lingerie into her jean jacket pocket just as Jacoby and the dog came back in the room.

"What ya doing?" Jacoby asked.

"Nothing."

Justin's one-word answer matched hers.

"Don't look like nothing."

Jacoby moved to stand in front of her, the dog still at his side. He planted his little feet and crossed his arms over his chest, his bear caught in between. Gina's heart softened as she looked down at her pint-size protector.

She raised her gaze to Justin, praying he understood. The blank look on his face told her he didn't.

"Jacoby, I didn't hear any water running while you were in the bathroom," she asked. "Did you forget to wash your hands?"

He looked at her over his shoulder. "Huh?"

"It's important to wash your hands every time you go to the bathroom."

"It is?"

Gina nodded. "Why don't you go— Or better yet, how about a bath before you head to bed?"

Jacoby shook his head. "He doesn't have a bathtub."

She looked back at Justin. "You don't?"

"It's a stand-up shower."

"But it does have two places where the water comes out," Jacoby added. "And one is just my size."

"I put in a regular shower head and a handheld," Justin leveled one hand at his waist. "You know, at hip level?"

She locked down the image of Justin standing naked in his shower, water hitting his skin from both angles, before it even had a chance to spring to life.

Gina turned her attention back to the boy. "Ah, okay. A shower, then?"

"I guess so, if I hafta."

"Yes, you have to," Justin said, reaching for the battered pillowcase near the chair. "You got clean clothes in here?"

Jacoby got to it first and grabbed the bag, holding it close to his chest. "I got pajamas."

Justin backed away, hands held high in surrender. He looked at her and she nodded for him to continue, hoping he saw it as encouragement.

"Why don't you head into the bathroom and get undressed and I'll get the water set for you?"

"Okay." Jacoby headed back toward the doorway.

Jack started for the boy, but Gina grabbed his collar. "You stay here. I think that room is going to be crowded enough."

"You gonna be here when I'm done?" Jacoby turned back to ask.

She didn't dare look at Justin or her watch. "If you'd like me to be."

The boy nodded vigorously.

"Then I'll—" she patted Jack's head "—we'll be here."

Jacoby headed for the bathroom again.

Justin followed, then stopped and faced her. "What was all that? Him standing between us?"

Gina moved closer and looked around Justin to make

sure the boy wasn't listening. "I think he was protecting me. Maybe something he's done in the past? For his mom?"

Justin nodded, but remained silent for a long moment. "You don't have to stay."

"I told him I would."

A sharp pain pierced her chest when Justin didn't reply but walked away. She ignored it, refusing to decide if it was a result of Justin's or Jacoby's actions. She turned away, heard a door open, then close, and a few minutes later the rush of running water.

A low whimper from Jack had her reaching out to scratch his head. "Don't worry, pal. We'll stick around, at least for a little while."

She looked around the room. Not the best layout for a little boy who obviously needed a good night's sleep. Hanging her jean jacket carefully on a hook by the door, she pushed up her sleeves and went to work.

Any bedrooms the cabin had must be down the same hallway that led to the bathroom, but she figured they had to be uninhabitable if Justin was sleeping out here. It took only a few minutes for her to shake out the sleeping bags, thick quilts and pillows on the floor and with the stuff she'd brought, make up twin sleeping pallets in front of the fire.

She moved the power tools to the far wall and stacked leftover pieces of cut wood into an empty box. A broom she found helped clean up the scarred wood floors. The night-light was plugged in and the kitchen lights and floor lamp turned off. Jack circled three times before curling up at the end of one of the pallets, putting his head on his paws.

"Don't get too comfortable," she huffed, pointing a finger at the mutt. "I need to get you back to your mama soon."

He just closed his eyes and started snoring.

"What have you done?"

She whirled around. Justin stood behind her, his T-shirt,

jeans and hair all varying levels of wet. "What happened to you?"

"Jacoby kept opening the shower curtain. I think he was afraid I was going to go through his pillowcase." He ran a hand through his hair, pushing it off his face, except for one piece that fell back onto his forehead. "You haven't answered my question. What happened out here?"

She clenched her hands together, determined not to fix that wayward lock. "I just— He's exhausted. You must be, as well. I figured if things were ready when you two got back out here it would be easier for him to fall asleep."

"I can handle laying out a few blankets."

"I'm not saying you can't. I was only trying— Hey, Jacoby."

Face pink and shiny clean from the hot shower, the little boy's features clearly showed his exhaustion as he walked into the room, dragging his pillowcase behind him.

"Why don't you crawl between the blankets over here with Jack?" she said, ignoring Justin's pointed look. "Would you like to read a book before you go to sleep?"

The boy stilled for a moment, before he shook his head. He stumbled past Justin, tucked the pillowcase under the top corner of the sleeping bag and crawled inside, hugging his stuffed bear. Jack scooted up to stretch out next to him and Jacoby wrapped one arm across the dog's shaggy belly.

"I think Jack wants to spend the night." Bending over, Gina gave the dog a quick pat. "Is that okay with you, Jacoby?"

Jacoby nodded, but Gina noticed his half-closed eyes were trained on her hair. He reached out and traced a tiny finger along a strand of curls. "Pink. I like it."

Her heart squeezed in her chest. She opened her mouth to reply, but the sound of a throat clearing stopped her.

Jacoby's eyes widened and he looked past Gina's shoulder. "Can he...can Jack...stay?"

Gina straightened and turned in time to see Justin's quick

nod. He then centered his gaze on her, his eyes hooded, as well, but not from fatigue. No, she guessed he wanted her out of here and the quicker the better. "I guess it's settled, then. I'll call Racy to tell her about Jack."

"I'll do that. He comes over all the time from their place."

"Well, I'll see myself out. Bye, Jacoby."

The boy was already fast asleep. She headed for the front door, grabbed her jacket and wrenched open the handle, stepping outside.

"Gina, wait, you dropped…"

She paused and turned around. Justin stood in the open doorway, a scrap of paper in his hand. She cringed as his eyes scanned the writing.

"What's this? 'Doctor's appointment, new clothes, register at school.'" He glared at her, his eyes sharp and piercing, his voice a low rumble. "You wrote this?"

She lifted her chin. "I'm just trying to—"

"Help. Yeah, I know. I think I've made it clear that I don't need your help."

"So I brought over a few groceries and swept your floors. It's not a big deal. Jacoby seems to be sleeping fine, so I guess I didn't upset him too much by stopping by. You, on the other hand, can't seem to wait to get rid of me. Why is that?"

His eyes narrowed. "Aren't you late for something?"

"Yes, I am. You know, you might want to try the words *thank you* on for size. If you think you can pull them on over that massive chip on your shoulder."

Gina spun away as he crumpled the paper in his fist. She stomped to the car and had the driver's side door open when she heard his front door close with a loud thud. Seconds later, she was behind the wheel and gunned the engine.

So much for good ideas.

Chapter Four

He was an idiot.

After spending last night thinking about the asinine way he'd reacted to Gina's list, Justin had come to that simple but honest conclusion beneath the hot spray of his morning shower.

One hundred percent, bona fide numbskull.

He stalked around the kitchen, grabbing the makings for pancakes and piling them on the center island. He wasn't mad about her list. Heck, not long after he'd stretched out next to the kid he had his own mental tally going. It'd stung that she thought he wouldn't be able to figure out the basic necessities for the boy, but that's not what caused his side trip into Boneheadland.

No, it was purely the fact all he'd wanted to do in that one moment on his front porch was pull her into his arms and cover her mouth with his.

One moment? How about many moments?

Like when she'd first arrived, standing at his front door

looking up at him, uncertainty in her eyes. Or in his darkened kitchen when embarrassment left a pretty pink blush on her face. Or how that blush deepened when he'd found her bra in the basket and realized she was wearing the matching panties.

Oh, yeah, he'd really wanted to kiss her then.

Hell, he'd wanted to kiss her from practically the first moment they met in his sister's office on the day he'd convinced Racy to hire him.

Then he found out she was the sheriff's younger sister.

That really put her out of his league, not that she and him were even in the same ballpark. He was a hundred percent all wrong for Gina Steele. Finding out her family connection should've quenched the ever-present fire burning in his gut, but it didn't. So he'd worked hard to stay away from her. Not the easiest thing to do with their tripping over each other at work. And holding her in his arms yesterday hadn't helped.

Justin slammed a mental door on his thoughts and focused on his plans for the day. He eyed the clock over the sink. After nine. He was usually up at dawn on weekends, but between trying to get used to the soft buzz of snores from the kid and thinking about a pair of wide blue eyes and soft pink lips—

Back to the plan.

Eating, laundry duty and shopping for a seven-year-old. He had no idea how long the kid was going to be with him, but seeing the ragged child-size toothbrush on the bathroom sink next to his told him there were certain things Jacoby needed right away. He also had to find a quiet moment to call the sheriff's office to see if Gage had found out anything more about Zoe or her whereabouts.

He grabbed an old-fashioned hand sifter and added flour, sugar, baking powder and salt. While cranking, he wondered if the kid liked anything special in his pancakes, like his personal favorites, bananas and chopped walnuts.

"Can I help?"

Justin looked over his shoulder. The kid stood at the counter on the living room side. His hair stood up in sharp angles, and his eyes were sleepy.

"Sure, but you should get dressed first. You got clean clothes in your bag?"

Jacoby nodded.

"Do you need help washing up?"

This time he shook his head but continued to stand there.

"Then go ahead and get changed."

After a slight hesitation he headed back toward the sleeping bag where Jack still lay, his tail thumping wildly against the fabric. The kid had waited for permission to go to the bathroom last night, too.

It took Justin back to his time behind bars when everything from eating to taking a leak required an okay from someone with a uniform and a gun. Not an easy habit to break in the months since his release, and he still found himself sometimes wavering before making a decision as simple as grabbing a bottle of water while slaving over a hot stove.

That didn't explain why a little boy would act the same.

He shook his head to dispel the memory and concentrated on the dry batter. Minutes later, the kid walked into the kitchen wearing a stained T-shirt and a pair of jeans that almost reached his bare ankles, a hole ripped in one knee.

"Aren't your feet cold?" Justin asked.

Jacoby looked at Justin's own bare feet and shook his head.

"Okay, then. You hungry?"

He nodded.

"Here, hold this." Justin handed over the sifter and pulled up a step stool to the center island. "Stand up here so you can see what's going on."

While climbing to the top step, Jacoby tipped the sifter. A dusting of the dry ingredients floated to the floor. "Oh, no!"

Justin saw what happened, but was more surprised by the alarm on the kid's face. "Don't worry, we'll clean it up later."

He stepped over the mess and took the sifter away. The boy now stood at waist level to the counter and his eyes grew wide at the assortment of items sitting there.

"Wow, what's all this for?"

"Pancakes."

"You don't have frozen ones?" he asked.

Justin's chest tightened for a moment and he concentrated on tapping an egg on the counter, then opening it one-handed, its contents dripping into a separate smaller bowl. "Ah, no, this is how you make pancakes from scratch."

"What's scratch?"

Smiling, Justin reached toward the egg carton. "It means using fresh ingredients instead of premade. Here, ever crack one of these?"

Jacoby nodded and grabbed for the two brown eggs. Both shells shattered from the boy's overzealous grip and egg sprayed onto the edge of the counter. Automatic reflexes had Justin reaching out, but the slippery ooze fell through his fingers and the yolks landed on the top of his foot with a one-two splat.

Jacoby let loose with a four-letter curse. Stunned by the boy's outburst, Justin just stood there. The boy smacked his hand over his mouth and the bright sheen of tears filled his eyes.

"Please don't be mad," he pleaded, dropping his hand and clenching a tiny fist to his chest. "I didn't mean it! I didn't mean to say that and I didn't mean to drop— I didn't! I'm sorry!"

"Hey, slow down—"

"I do this all the time. My mom gets so mad when I make a mess. I'll clean it up, I promise."

Jacoby started to scramble down from the step stool. It rocked to one side and Justin reached out to stop him from falling, grabbing him by the arm.

The kid cried out. Justin quickly released him, latching on to the stool instead. He had no idea what was going on, but things were going downhill and fast.

"Jacoby, it's no big deal. I'm not mad."

The boy froze in place, then looked up at him. He sniffed. "Are you lying?"

Geez, what had this kid lived through? Justin straightened. "No, I'm not lying."

Huge tears and a wary disbelief filled the boy's eyes. Justin had to do something before this situation got out of hand. But what?

"You know, you're the one who should be mad," he blurted.

The wariness took over full-time in those small eyes. "Me?"

Justin prayed he was doing the right thing as he reached for the almost-empty flour sifter. Seconds later, the leftovers landed in puffs of white on the boy's head.

"Sure, you're the one with flour in his hair."

"Hey!"

He surprised the kid, that's for sure. Wiping the inside of the sifter with his fingers, he flicked the dust at the boy's chest. "And now it's on your shirt."

The kid looked down, then grinned. "No fair. Mine was an accident."

Justin smiled and kicked out an egg-covered foot, his aim on target as a plop of egg yolk landed on Jacoby's toes. "Oops!"

And just like that, a food fight was born.

Everything on the island was up for grabs including the

chopped walnuts and mashed bananas. Pancake ingredients were tossed through the air and although Justin had the height advantage, he made sure the kid got a few direct hits.

Little boy laughter filled the air and Justin was surprised to find himself joining in as he alternated between chasing and allowing himself to be chased around the island. They both slipped a few times on the messy floor, but it wasn't until he spotted Jacoby eyeing the carton of eggs that he called a halt to the fun.

"Don't even think about it." He lifted the carton high overhead.

"Aw, come on!"

Justin placed the eggs on top of the refrigerator. "Yeah, like I'm crazy enough to let you nail me with raw eggs… again."

The kid's smile slipped a bit. "I didn't mean to—"

"I know," Justin interjected. "It was an accident, that's all. Stuff happens, ya know?"

Jacoby nodded.

"How about we get you in the shower and I'll clean up here? Then we'll eat and head into town. I have a few errands to run, including a stop at the Suds Bucket."

"Where?"

"It's a place to do laundry." Justin tossed out the pancake mix and reached for a roll of paper towels. "Don't you have clothes that need washing?"

Jacoby dropped his head but nodded. "Some."

"You got anything else that's clean to change into?"

"Yeah, I think so."

Justin mentally added new clothes to his ever-growing list. The kid obviously needed them considering the condition of his current outfit, even before the food fight. He added a backpack to the list, too. If anything needed a good washing it was that pillowcase. Or better yet, it should be tossed in the closest trash can.

He thought again about Gina's list.

Should he take the boy to the local clinic just to make sure there weren't any health issues? And at seven years old, Jacoby must be in the first grade. Or was it the second? Justin had no idea how long the kid was going to be with him, but he should be in school.

He ignored the ache in his stomach and quickly cleaned up his feet so as not to track the remains of their food fight through the rest of the cabin.

"You mind if I give you a lift to the bathroom?" he asked, remembering how Jacoby had cried out earlier when he'd touched him. He didn't even want to think about where that reaction came from. "We need to keep the mess here in the kitchen."

"You mean like a piggyback ride?"

Justin shrugged. "Sure, if you want."

The kid smiled and the ache eased a little. Justin refused to think about why as he hoisted Jacoby onto his back.

"And then Gina cleaned up the living room," Jacoby said before shoving a ketchup-drowned French fry into his mouth. "It needed it, too. The place was a mess."

"Hey!" Justin protested as his sister grinned.

Racy sat next to the kid and opposite Justin in a window booth at Sherry's Diner. They'd run into her after stopping in for a late lunch.

It still surprised Justin how easy it'd been to rebuild a relationship with her after his years away. It meant a lot to him that she'd believed him when he vowed he was ready to turn his life around. Unlike their older brother who was back behind bars. Despite being freed along with Justin, Billy had gotten involved with the drug scene again, resulting in a fire that destroyed their childhood home and a failed attempt at extorting money from Racy.

"Was it that bad?" she asked.

"No." Justin and Jacoby spoke in unison.

"I was kidding." Jacoby concentrated on his fries again. "It's a nice place."

"Gina just moved some boxes and swept up the dust." Justin continued when Racy raised an eyebrow in his direction. "Then she laid out the pillows and blankets."

"And she let Jack stay," Jacoby added.

"I let Jack stay," Justin countered.

"But it was Gina's idea."

"Actually, it was her idea." Justin pointed at his sister. "Gina said you suggested she bring that mutt along on her little charity visit."

"You liked sleeping with Jack?" Racy looked down at Jacoby, ignoring Justin's comment.

The boy nodded, his mouth now busy sucking on the straw in his glass of milk.

"My husband is still getting used to sharing his king-size bed." Racy smiled. "He tends to sleep all stretched out while laying his head on the nearest pillow. Jack, that is."

Jacoby laughed as he put his glass back on the table. Seconds later, he pointed at the window. "Look! It's Gina!"

The boy jumped to his knees and spun around to look over the back of the booth. Seconds later, Gina walked in. Jacoby scooted from his seat and darted across the diner toward the front counter.

"Hey!" Justin called out, but the kid was already at Gina's side.

"Wow, he's certainly taken with Gina." Racy turned back from watching the two of them. "She's all he's talked about since we sat down."

"Tell me about it. She was at the cabin less than an hour last night, but it's like she's woven a spell over him." Justin jabbed at his lunch with a fork. "Was it one of those full moons at twilight last night or something?"

Racy grinned. "I think that's for vampires and werewolves, not witches."

"Whatever. She's got the boy wrapped around her finger."

"And quite a few older boys, if the attention she's getting at The Blue Creek means anything," Racy offered with a wink. "For someone who started out so shy and reserved, she certainly has blossomed in the last few months. Don't you think?"

Justin didn't rise to the bait.

He'd expected his sister to warn him off Gina months ago, but that advice never came. And once the news broke about Racy and Gage's secret wedding in Vegas last year, an event they'd recreated for family and friends here in Destiny on Valentine's Day, his independent and sassy sister transformed into the picture of love and marital bliss.

Not that he faulted her for her ongoing joy. She deserved to be happy after all she'd dealt with in her life. But lately, she'd been making noises about wanting him to be as happy as she was, no matter how many times Justin told her his life was fine just as it was.

Or it had been. Until the kid showed up and now everything was turned upside down and twisted inside out. He'd been getting his act together, but that didn't mean he had any plans for falling in love.

Him and happily ever after didn't mix.

"Don't look now—" Racy glanced over her shoulder again "—but your witch is heading this way, thanks to a very determined little boy."

Justin couldn't stop himself. His eyes locked with Gina's. He read surprise and annoyance in her gaze, but also an unwillingness to pull free from the small hand tugging her toward their table.

He forced himself to look away, but his gaze caught on her hair, straight and smooth today versus the sexy, curly mess from last night. The pink streak was still there and it matched the bright pink of her fleece jacket. Black jeans hugged her curves and she wore the same cowboy boots from last night.

Not that he'd noticed. Much.

"Look who's here!" Jacoby announced when they arrived at the table.

"Hi, Gina," Racy said.

"Hey, boss."

Justin concentrated on the remains of his lunch until he felt the sharp nudge of Racy's boot to his shin. He glared at his sister from beneath half-closed eyelids, but she only returned his stare, her mouth flat in a hard line.

He suppressed a sigh and turned to the girl he'd managed to keep out of his head most of the afternoon. Until now.

"Hi."

Her blue eyes flashed the same sparks they'd held last night on his front porch. "Hi yourself."

"Gina's got food coming so I told her she could wait with us," Jacoby said with a wide grin. Just as quickly as the smile appeared, it vanished. "Oh, shoot, I'll be right back. Gina, you can sit over there."

"Hey, where are you going?" Justin asked, overlooking the fact the kid offered the empty spot next to him.

"The bathroom. You said when I had to go I could just go."

"At the cabin, sure, but out in public—well, you can't just take off."

Jacoby tilted his head to one side. "Why?"

Justin didn't know how to answer that. He looked at his sister, but it was Gina who spoke first.

"Because we'd be worried," she said. "You need to let Justin, or any adult you're with, know where you're going, especially if you plan to go off alone."

Caution, an emotion Justin had witnessed many times

since he met the boy, filled the child's eyes. He looked from Gina back to him. "You'd be worried about me?"

He could feel Gina's steady gaze on him, but he kept his focus on the kid. "Ah, yeah, sure."

"Cool. Can I go to the bathroom now?"

Justin nodded, pointing out the entrance to the restrooms. The kid raced off and a long silence filled the air.

"Oh, Justin, I meant to tell you." Racy snapped her fingers. "Nikki from the bar said she has a twin bed you can have for free if you can pick it up."

"A what?"

"A bed. For Jacoby. He can't camp out on the living room floor forever."

"Wow, that's so nice of Nikki," Gina gushed, crossing her arms over her chest. "But I thought you weren't interested in anyone's help?"

He glared at her, trying to ignore how her actions caused a hint of lace and the smooth skin of her cleavage to appear.

"Then again, Jacoby is going to need a decent bed to sleep in," she continued in a syrupy-sweet voice. "But I'm sure you already thought of that."

He hadn't.

Simple things like sneakers and a toothbrush, sure. But a place to sleep? Hell, he still hadn't gotten the bed he planned to use for himself put together yet.

"No, I haven't thought about getting the kid a bed."

"Well, problem solved. You can pick it up on your way home." Racy wore a quizzical look as her gaze shot between him and Gina. "Aren't you going to sit?"

"Ah—"

"Here, take my place." Racy stacked her dishes to one side before sliding out of the booth. "I need to get going. Tell Jacoby I'll see him later. Bye!"

Gina stepped aside to let Racy get by, but remained standing next to the booth, arms crossed.

"Waiting for an engraved invitation?"

Okay, that wasn't necessary, but at least it got her to sit. She dropped into the booth, her hands now shoved into the pockets of her jacket. An awkward silence stretched between them, so Justin said the first thing that popped into his head.

"I was an ass."

That got her attention. "Yes, you were."

"I'm not talking about just now." He gave his head a quick shake and reached for his coffee. "Last night, too. On my porch."

Gina pulled her hands from her jacket and laid them on the table, her silver-tipped nails playing with a stack of unused napkins. "Yes, you were," she repeated.

The apology he knew he should give stuck in his throat. "Do you think he's okay in the bathroom alone?" he said instead.

Gina glanced across the crowded diner. "He should be fine. You can see the doorway from here."

He looked in the direction of the restrooms again, this time noticing their booth seemed to be getting quite a bit of attention from the diner's other patrons.

"Is it just me," he said, his voice low as he turned back to her, "or are people staring?"

Without turning her head, her gaze darted to the other tables and booths around them. "Well, it's not too often a stranger comes to town only to disappear after leaving a child behind. I guess Jacoby is news."

"And of all people for the kid to be stuck with, it's me."

Like he and Gina hadn't given the town enough to talk about over the last few months? Now he'd have the entire population watching his every move with the kid.

"So, you two went shopping?" Gina asked, filling the silence. "I noticed Jacoby's new clothes."

"We hit Wal-Mart after dropping Jack off at Racy's." Justin

found himself grateful for the change in topic. "Who knew it'd take over two hours to shop for one little kid."

"I'm guessing he needed quite a few things. Was the rest of his stuff as bad as that outfit he had on when he first showed up?"

"Pretty much. We just finished another couple of hours at the laundromat." He put the coffee mug down. "I washed everything he had in that ratty pillowcase of his, including the case. I tried to convince him to throw it out, but he wouldn't."

Gina's jaw dropped. "Justin, you didn't."

"What?"

"That bag, no matter its condition, and what little he might have inside, is all he has. Of course he'd want to keep it. You should know that better than anyone."

Geez, the girl was good for a quick swift kick in the butt.

"I didn't think—" He slumped against the seat cushion and pinched the bridge of his nose. "How stupid can I be?"

Gina was right. He should know better because he'd walked out of prison with his entire life's possessions in a cardboard box. All he owned now was a growing collection of books, a few power tools, a beat-up truck and some meager household items.

Damn, who knew he and the kid had so much in common?

"You're not stupid." Gina pointed at the pillowcase next to Justin. "Did you see if there was anything in there that might help you find his mother?"

"No. I got him a new backpack, too, but he only used it to hold his stuff while the pillowcase was washed. Then he loaded everything back into the case, including his bear, which he refused to allow anywhere near the suds."

Justin straightened and glanced at the restrooms again.

"Hell, I'm surprised he left the table without them, the pillowcase or the bear."

"Has he talked about his mother much?"

Justin shook his head and found himself leaning forward. With a low voice, he relayed the events with the eggs and the food fight from this morning. He didn't know why he felt compelled to share the story with Gina, but it just fell from his lips.

"That's so sad." Gina inched forward and put her hand over his, giving him a gentle squeeze when he finished speaking. "But Jacoby seems fine now. I think you handled the situation well."

She did?

Justin didn't know how to respond, to her compliment or the warmth of her touch. All he wanted was to flip his hand over and capture hers in his grasp.

Damn, he was in trouble here. He really owed her that apology now. Before he had a chance to speak, a waitress came by with her order.

Gina snatched her hand away and reached for the large paper bag. "Well, this is my food. I need to get going."

"Gina—"

She scooted out of the booth just as Jacoby returned.

"Where ya going?" he asked.

"Ah, I have to leave. My brother and sister are waiting for their food, but I'll see you soon, okay?"

Justin saw Jacoby nod as the boy stood there and watched her walk away. Justin found himself doing the same.

There was no way he'd get in that bed.

No way. No how.

Jacoby squeezed Clem tighter and kept his eyes glued on the small television sitting on the floor next to the fireplace. His eyeballs were scratchy. It felt like he was pulling a warm blanket over 'em when they closed, but he fought to keep 'em open.

If he fell asleep he was sure Justin would pick him up and carry him to the small bedroom. He'd put him beneath the covers. Then he'd leave.

And Jacoby would be alone.

He didn't want to be alone. But he wasn't going to tell Justin that. He'd probably think Jacoby was a baby or something.

He wasn't.

It's just that there were a lot of strange noises and the windows in that room didn't have anything covering them.

He wished Jack was here. Maybe if the dog slept next to him in that bed he wouldn't be afraid.

Because he liked it here.

The cabin was nice and warm, there was always food and he liked that he didn't have to ask first when he wanted something to eat or to go to the bathroom.

His mama used to make him do that sometimes, ask before he could do anything.

And sometimes the answer would be no.

She'd say no over and over until he'd finally stopped asking. Then he'd pray he wouldn't have an accident or that his tummy would stop growling until she changed her mind.

Which she always did, eventually. Then she'd cry and say she was sorry and she wouldn't do it again.

But she would.

But for the past two days, Justin had been the one asking him what he wanted. First, the new clothes, including two pairs of sneakers because they were buy one get one half off. Then he got to pick the color of his new toothbrush and finally the backpack that sat empty near the bookcase.

He liked the backpack. It was blue and had a cool swirly design on it and none of those babyish cartoon guys. But except for using it to hold his stuff while Justin insisted on washing his pillowcase, it sat empty.

Jacoby didn't know how long he was going to be here. His mama had said he was going to stay with Justin and Justin was going to be his dad, but he wasn't sure he believed her.

So he'd keep using his pillowcase. He wasn't going to use anything he didn't really need, like that backpack and the second set of sneakers.

Or that bed.

But he would like to see Gina again.

A sharp pain caused his belly to hurt and he hugged Clem tighter to his chest. Was it because he'd rather see Gina again than his mom?

But Gina was nice. And she smelled good, too, like his favorite cookie, snickerdoodles, and she didn't talk to him like he was a baby.

Maybe he should ask if she could come over again.

Then again, Justin had gotten a funny look on his face whenever Jacoby asked about her.

Maybe he didn't like Gina. Naw, Justin would hafta be stupid not to like Gina.

Wouldn't he?

Chapter Five

It had been a hell of a weekend. Justin was ready to collapse and the kid who'd been his constant companion for the last forty-eight hours was halfway to snoozeville himself.

Trouble was, the kid refused to go to bed.

Correction, the kid refused to sleep in the twin bed they'd set up in the second bedroom this afternoon.

Just like he'd done last night.

He hadn't thought anything of it when the boy had asked if he could sleep in front of the fire like he'd done his first night at the cabin. At the time, the bed had been in pieces. They'd spent most of today cleaning both bedrooms, getting rid of years of accumulated junk and debris from the previous owner. Then they put the kid's bed together, along with a matching dresser, but the boy wanted nothing to do with the room.

Justin didn't get it.

And to top it off, he continued to ask when Gina was coming by to see them again.

Running into her yesterday at the diner had left a hard lump in Justin's chest that still hadn't gone away. He didn't know if it was from the fact he never got to apologize for the way he'd talked to her Friday night or maybe it came from the phone call he'd made to Gage late yesterday afternoon.

Despite the sheriff's inquiries, there were still no leads on Zoe's whereabouts.

How could a woman walk away from her child? Didn't she wonder if her son was okay? Wasn't she worried he didn't have any idea how to take care of a kid? Then again, considering the boy's strange behavior this weekend, maybe having Zoe out of his life wasn't necessarily a bad thing.

But where did that leave Justin?

"Are you mad at Gina?"

Jacoby's question pulled him from his thoughts. He looked down at the boy who'd rolled over to face him. "What? No, why'd you ask that?"

"You look mad. Just like you did when I asked if she was going to come visit again."

He relaxed his facial features. "I'm not mad."

Jacoby shrugged and turned away. He clutched his bear closer to his chest. "You should be nicer to her."

"To Gina?" Justin dropped to the sleeping bag, ignoring how his cell phone pressed into his groin. "Why's that?"

The boy shrugged again. "My teacher said boys are supposed to be nice to girls. Even if they can't play ball and they giggle a lot."

Did Gina giggle? No, her laugh was low, smoky and smooth, much like a fine, aged whiskey. He remembered the first time he'd heard it, less than an hour after they'd met. It had brought to mind Hollywood's leading ladies of the '40s from those old movies he'd always liked to watch. The sound didn't fit her age, but he'd learned Gina wasn't like most girls her age in a lot of ways.

He shifted. "Ah, you should be getting to bed."

"I am in bed."

Justin sighed. He really needed some alone time. Time to think about what he was going to do next in this crazy twist his life had taken. "I mean in your own room."

"I'm not...sleepy." Jacoby continued to face away from him, but Justin heard him yawn. "My mom lets me stay up as late as I want."

That was the first time he'd mentioned his mother all weekend. "Really?"

The kid's head bobbed up and down. "Sometimes she and Miss Mazie would both be passed out and I'd stay up for hours watching television."

Passed out? "You mean they fell asleep?"

"Well, they'd drink and laugh. Miss Mazie loved to drink. And my mom would smoke these funny-smelling cigarettes and they'd make her sleepy."

Justin held back a groan. "Does Miss Mazie have a last name?"

"I don't know. I just called her Miss Mazie."

"Think hard. Did she ever tell you her name?"

"Now you really sound mad."

"I'm not mad," Justin repeated, slumping back against the pillows. He'd let it go for now. "I'm confused. Why won't you go sleep in that bed? You were so excited when we put it together."

"I thought Gina might come over and see it first."

"Gina, again? What made you think that?"

"Because I know if you said it was okay, she would come!" Jacoby jumped up. "I'm not going to sleep in that dumb old bed or in that dumb old room, and you can't make me."

Before Justin could move, the kid took off. By the time he got to his feet and followed, the bathroom door slammed shut. A sharp click sounded.

Damn! He'd forgotten about the lock. Maybe it was so old

it wouldn't catch. He grabbed the handle and twisted. No such luck. "Jacoby, open this door."

"No!"

Justin shook the handle. "Open this door right now."

"No!" The boy's voice rose another octave. "I'm not openin' nothin' until Gina comes."

Oh, hell no. There was no way he was calling her.

Justin took a step back and looked at the door. Solid oak, probably close to a hundred years old with hinges on the inside. Taking a screwdriver to the original hardware was unacceptable.

His fingers curled and he was tempted to puncture his words with a few sharp raps on the wood. "Jacoby, you need to open this door…now."

Silence. Justin relaxed his hand. Scaring the kid wasn't going to help. Instead, he sighed and dug into his pocket for his phone.

"Are you still a virgin?"

Gina froze midbrush, the minty froth of her toothpaste causing her to gag. She turned to find her younger sister, Giselle, standing in the doorway of her bathroom.

Clenching on to the toothbrush with her teeth, she spoke around the bristles. "Whad did yuz sway?"

"You heard me."

Giselle moved back into the bedroom and dropped to Gina's bed, rolling to her stomach so that she faced away from her. Gina shot a look at her bedroom door, grateful to find it closed.

She rinsed her mouth and tossed her toothbrush into the cup on the sink. Wiping her hands on the closest towel, she did her best to wipe the shock from her face, as well.

"You want to run that by me again?" She joined her sister on the bed, a stack of pillows at her back.

"Do I have to say it again?"

"No, but how about you tell me why you're asking?" Gina nudged her sister's jean-clad thigh.

Giselle offered a dramatic sigh, something she did often and with great skill, and flopped over onto her back.

Two months away from graduating high school, she'd celebrated her eighteenth birthday, along with her twin brother, Garrett, just a few weeks ago. Having left home when the twins were in the first grade to attend a private school for the gifted, Gina wasn't close to her younger siblings. She had come back on breaks and vacations, but she and the twins were always more polite strangers than family.

When she'd returned home for good this time, she'd been determined to change that. She and Giselle had spent a lot of time together, shopping and going to movies, but this was the first time one of their girl talks had ever approached such a serious subject.

"Hello?" Gina prodded.

"I was just wondering because…" Giselle's voice was soft, her gaze glued to the ceiling. "Well, I'm eighteen now and so many of my friends aren't virgins anymore. I'm not… completely innocent, but I'm still— Were you a virgin when you graduated high school?"

"I was fifteen." Gina offered a smile. "So, yeah, I was."

Giselle snorted. "Like age means anything nowadays." Then she looked at her. "But you're not now, right?"

"I'm also five years older than you."

Giselle sighed and grabbed one of the pillows, hugging it to her chest. "Stefan and I have been exclusive since the prom last year. He's wanted to—you know—for a while, but I've been holding off. I'm not sure I'm ready."

"If you're not ready, you're not ready. Seems pretty simple to me."

"What if I'm ready in my heart, but my head keeps telling me to hold off?"

Gina fingered the hem of her plaid flannel pants, her

standard pajamas along with her favorite University of Notre Dame sweatshirt. "Have you tried talking to Mom about this?"

Her sister's blue eyes widened. "Are you nuts? Mom is still buying me dolls for Christmas."

"It was an ornament for the tree and you've been collecting that series for years," Gina said. "I think Mom would be understanding…and helpful."

Giselle rolled her eyes. "Mom and I had 'the talk' back when I was in junior high, and it's been a while since she was a teenager. Besides, you said I could come to you about anything, remember?"

Yes, she'd said those exact words. "Okay. So tell me again what you're really asking?"

"How will I know when I'm ready? How did you know? I mean, you aren't still a virgin, right?"

Gina studied her sister's serious gaze. She saw curiosity and also a genuine need for help with comprehending the crazy world of adulthood she was moving into. "No, but it was only last summer I was with someone for the first time."

"At King's College in London?"

Memories from last year flooded back, more bittersweet than painful, but a tender wound still lingered. Her mother had told her things would get better when she held Gina in her arms, not asking questions while Gina cried. She'd told her in time the hurt would fade and then she'd be able to deal with whatever had brought her home to Destiny.

She'd been right, but still, Gina found herself coming to terms with the way her first love affair had ended. "I met Geoffrey my first week of classes, and he literally swept me off my feet. He looked like Jude Law, right down to the accent and he was even smarter than me.… I was in heaven."

Giselle released a small sigh. "He sounds wonderful. So you two hadn't dated long before you…you know."

"No, we didn't. It was a whirlwind romance, if you want

the cliché term. He pulled me out of my shell and showed me a whole new world full of fun and laughter and…passion." Gina pulled one of the other pillows into her lap and held it tight. "You've got to remember, I didn't date much in high school or college—*much* meaning not at all. Most of my classmates were at least three years older than me. Studying was my number-one concern. I know now that I used studying as a way to hide, concentrating on the books instead of meeting people."

Gina paused, her chest tight with the remembered joy and heartache Geoffrey had brought into her life. "When I went to England I was hoping to change that. Geoffrey seemed to be everything I was looking for."

More than what she was looking for, it turned out, and not in a good way.

"But you left here in June and your fellowship was supposed to last a year. You surprised us by coming home last December. So that's over now? Your relationship with Geoffrey?"

Gina nodded. What she'd had with the charming, British associate professor was more than over. How could it be anything different considering he'd been in no position to start a relationship in the first place?

"So have you met anyone since you've been back?" Giselle asked. "Other than Justin Dillon, I mean."

Her sister's words caused Gina's throat to squeeze closed. It took a hard swallow and a gulp of air before she could speak. "Wh-what makes you say that?"

"Well, everyone knows you spent the night at his place a few months ago. It's not like you two are even close to being in a relationship. So, what was that? A walk on the wild side?"

Gina held back a groan. How was she going to explain that night? Maybe by telling the truth?

Her cell phone chimed, interrupting her thoughts. She

reached for it. Unfamiliar number. Maybe it was someone from work looking to trade a shift. "Ah, let me get this and we'll finish… Hello?"

"Gina?"

Her breath caught, and again she lost the ability to speak. It was as if thinking about the man had caused him to dial her number. And how had he gotten her number?

"It's Justin."

As if she didn't recognize the unhurried, seductive timbre of his voice. She nodded and then realized what she did. "Ah, hi…hello."

"Look, I hate to do this, but I wonder if you'd—" He broke off and heaved a deep sigh. A sigh so sexy that Gina's toes curled.

"Would you mind coming out to the cabin?"

Would she mind— Her gaze flicked to the clock radio on her bedside table. It was nearly eleven o'clock. "Now?"

"I know it's late, but— Dammit!" The frustration in his voice was clear, and she pictured him tunneling his fingers through his hair as he paced. Justin struck her as a pacing kind of guy.

"Gina…" He paused for a moment. "I need your help."

A long silence filled the air.

"Hello? You still there?"

She opened her mouth to speak but nothing came out. Justin was asking for help. From her.

"Y-yes, I'm here. What's going on?"

"Jacoby's— Well, he's upset and he's asking for you."

Oh, the poor kid. His entire world had been turned upside down in the last forty-eight hours. And no matter the reasons his mother had for doing what she did, Jacoby must be missing her.

"I'll be there as soon as I can," she said.

After promising Giselle she'd keep the topic just between them and to finish their talk later, Gina changed her clothes, gave a quick explanation to her mother and headed out the door. Less than twenty minutes later she was parking her car next to Justin's truck.

He held open the screen door as she got to the porch and a sense of déjà vu swept over her as she stepped inside. The cardboard boxes were gone and a variety of books, from oversize hardbound textbooks to paperbacks, filled the shelves which flanked the fireplace. The power tools, scraps of wood and the oversize toolbox she'd barely been able to lift had disappeared, too.

But those changes paled in comparison to the sight of Justin, wearing a washed-out Destiny High Blue Devils T-shirt and faded jeans, his features etched with worry.

"What's going on?" she asked.

He pointed to a doorway on the opposite side of the room. "Jacoby's locked himself in the bathroom. He won't open the door. Hell, he won't even talk to me."

"Why'd he do that?"

"I don't know." Justin pushed the wayward locks of hair off his forehead with the back of one hand. The worry on his face had quickly morphed into exasperation. "I've been trying to get him in bed for over an hour, but he refuses. We spent all day cleaning the place and set up the bed, but he says he wants to sleep out here again."

Gina saw the sleeping bags laid out in front of the fire. "Are you planning to sleep out here?"

"Yeah, my bed's still missing a mattress."

"But you had a bed at your apartment."

Justin stilled, his gaze locked with hers, the chocolate brown of his eyes deepening.

Was he thinking about that night? How she'd tried to make him lie down after she'd followed him upstairs? How he'd insisted if she was going to stick around she should be the one to get some sleep? She'd been afraid he'd had a concussion, but when he'd taken the only chair, she'd had nowhere else to sit but on the rumpled bed. Eventually, she'd crawled beneath the covers to get warm and had indeed fallen asleep.

"I got rid of that bed when I moved here."

She didn't know what that meant, if it meant anything at all, but she refused to ask him to explain.

Moving toward the small hallway, she stopped in front of the only closed door. The other two, at opposite ends of the hall, stood open, leading to Jacoby's and Justin's bedrooms.

She knocked gently. "Jacoby? It's Gina. Are you okay?"

No reply. She tried again. "Hey, I heard you wanted to see me. Well, here I am. Can you come out?"

Still nothing. Gina looked over her shoulder at Justin, standing with his shoulder braced against the doorjamb. Then a click sounded and the door slowly opened. Jacoby stood inside, his bear at his side.

She dropped to her knees to meet his eyes. "Hey, there."

"Hey."

"So, what's going on?"

Jacoby looked over her shoulder at Justin. "He wants me to go to bed."

"It's late. Everyone should be in bed by now," Justin said.

"Aren't you tired?" Gina asked, drawing the boy's attention back to her. She dropped her purse to the floor and slipped out of her jacket.

"I'm not...tired."

"It looks like you two did a lot of work around here this weekend. I bet you were a big help. Can you show me what you two did?"

Jacoby nodded and stepped forward, but stopped when Justin straightened from the doorway. She handed her stuff to him. "Can you take these for me? And you know what I'd love right now? A cup of hot chocolate. Why don't you make some for all of us?"

Understanding dawned in his eyes as Justin took her things. "Sure. Three hot chocolates coming up."

After Justin headed back into the kitchen, Gina held out her hand. "Come on, Jacoby. It's okay."

His small fingers clamped on to hers. She rose and followed his lead into the living room. He showed her the bookshelves, and she listened as he explained about the shed outside the kitchen door where the tools were now locked up.

"Wow, you two worked hard today." The light from the fireplace danced off the still-unadorned, but freshly washed window panes that filled the two walls of the living room. "You even washed the windows."

"Yep." Jacoby smiled. "I did the ones on the bottom and Justin did the tops. We did every window out here and the ones in the bedrooms, too."

"Sounds like you made a good team."

"I even got to use his tools," Jacoby continued. "He showed me how to use a philly-head screwdriver."

"Phillips head," Justin said, joining them with a tray of steaming mugs that he placed on the counter separating the kitchen from the living room. "The hot chocolate needs to cool."

"So what did you use the screwdriver on?" Gina asked.

"We fixed some loose handles in the kitchen," Jacoby said. "And we put beds together, his and mine."

"Oh, I heard you were getting a bed, can I see it?"

Jacoby didn't do anything for a long moment, then he nodded and led Gina to the darkened room at one end of the hallway. A night-light shone in one corner.

"You can see better with the light on." Justin's arm brushed hers as he reached inside and flipped the switch.

An overhead light shone down on a twin-size bed made up with sheets, a pillow and one of the quilts Gina recognized from the living room. A small table sat next to the bed and a three-drawer dresser stood against one wall across from a closet.

"Wow, nice room. Nice bed, too." Gina entered. "Can I sit on it? Will it hold me, you think?"

Jacoby giggled and followed her. "Of course it will."

Gina sat and bounced a few times. "Looks like you did a good job, Jacoby. I think this bed could even hold your dad. If he could fit in it."

"N-no, he's too big. You should see his bed. It's huge."

Gina caught Jacoby's hesitation. Was it because she called Justin his dad? She looked up and found Justin still in the doorway, again with one shoulder braced and arms crossed over his chest. He returned her stare, his face devoid of any emotion.

She turned her focus back to Jacoby. "Well, he's a big guy."

Jacoby nodded, moving closer to the bed. He rubbed at the soft material of the faded quilt, but his gaze darted around the room, not looking at her or Justin.

"Hey, I bet that hot chocolate is ready." Gina looked at Justin again, but he'd already turned and walked away.

Silence filled the air, and she wondered what to say next. The room was a bit bare, but otherwise it seemed fine. She saw Jacoby's pillowcase sticking out from beneath the bed. "Would you like to read a story while we drink our hot chocolate?"

Jacoby shook his head, his eyes focused on the invisible pattern he traced on the quilt.

"It might help make you sleepy."

Her words triggered a yawn the boy couldn't hide.

"And this bed feels like a perfect place to have sweet dreams." She smoothed her hand over the pillow. "Don't you even want to try it out?"

Jacoby hesitated and then shook his head.

"I'll stay right here with you."

He looked unconvinced. "You will?"

"Sure." She rose and pulled back the blankets. "Why don't you and your bear climb up here and see how it feels?"

Justin returned with the tray full of mugs as Gina tucked the quilt around Jacoby, who leaned on the pillow now propped against the simple wooden headboard.

"Three hot chocolates," Justin said, stopping at the side of the bed. He looked from Jacoby to her, one corner of his mouth tilted into a small grin. "I hope you guys like marshmallows."

"Marshmallows are perfect." She ignored the fluttering in her stomach and handed the smallest of the three mugs to Jacoby. "Here you go. Careful, it's going to be warm."

She took one of the remaining mugs and sipped. "Hmm, good. Almost as good as having a bed to sleep in again, huh, Jacoby?"

"I wouldn't know," the boy mumbled, his gaze on the cup in his hands. "I've never had one before."

Gina's heart lurched. "Never had one what?"

Jacoby took a long swallow from the mug before he spoke. "My own bed. Or even my own room."

She blinked hard to fight back the sudden stinging in her eyes. The surprise on Justin's face told her this was the first time he'd heard this. "Aren't you lucky, then?" Gina kept her voice light. "You get both in one night."

Jacoby leaned in close, his small brown eyes locked with hers. "I always wanted my own bed. Usually I'd have to share one with my mamma or sleep on the floor in a smelly, old sleeping bag," he whispered. "But I didn't know…"

His voice faded, and when he didn't continue, she asked, "Didn't know what, sweetie?"

"How scary it would be."

Chapter Six

Justin couldn't believe it. That's the reason Jacoby wouldn't go to sleep?

He thought the kid would be excited about finally having his own bed and his own room. Growing up, Justin had often craved a room of his own. Then again, there had been times when he'd been like Jacoby, when he'd been glad to know his brother Billy Joe was there in the dark with him.

But what in the heck were he and Gina going to do now? The night-light wasn't going to solve this kind of issue.

He took a sip from his mug, meeting Gina's eyes over the rim. The lukewarm chocolaty sweetness pooled on his tongue. Powerless to look away from the compassion he saw in those blue depths, he knew calling her had been the right thing to do.

For Jacoby.

Gina looked at the boy again. "So, what can we do to make it less scary?"

"You could spend the night, too."

The kid's words caused the mouthful of chocolate to rush down Justin's throat. It took a couple of fist thumps to his chest before he could breathe again. He dared a glance at Gina, but her gaze was glued to the marshmallows in her mug.

"Ah, no, I don't think that's possible," she said.

"Why not?"

Yeah, Gina, why not?

Whoa, where'd that come from?

As if she could read Justin's mind, she looked at him, peering beneath long, dark lashes, and that pink blush he'd seen many times before was back on her cheeks.

Bewitching and innocent, what a combination.

"I have my own bed at home," she said softly and then broke the spell by turning back to Jacoby. "And I have my own teddy bear who will wonder where I've gotten to." She smiled and touched the kid's stuffed bear on its black button nose.

"You have a teddy bear?" Jacoby asked. "Really?"

"Really. Now, tell me what you don't like about the room. Maybe we can do something about it."

Jacoby shrugged. "I don't know."

Justin pushed away his musings about Gina. He was sure the kid had something in mind, and equally sure he wasn't about to admit it aloud.

"Hmmm, I wonder if having curtains on the windows might make it easier to fall asleep," Gina said, before taking another sip of her hot chocolate.

Curtains?

Justin studied the room's two windows. They looked like all the others in the cabin. Less than a month old, double-paned for better insulation and uncovered. He preferred them that way. After spending seven years never looking out a pane of glass that didn't include bars or security threads running through it, he needed to see the surrounding woods without obstruction.

"There's nothing out there but trees and the lake," he said.

"And animals," Jacoby added softly.

"It's going to bother you if a deer or a raccoon sees you in your pajamas?"

The kid hesitated and then jerked his head in a quick nod. Justin started to roll his eyes, but a stern look from Gina stopped him.

"The scenery is beautiful, but don't you have a couple of sheets or drop cloths you could nail over the windows?" she asked.

Her voice was soft, but Justin didn't miss the underlying firm tone. He opened his mouth to protest, but all it took was a simple tilt of her head and he caved.

"Let me see what I can find."

Five minutes later he was back with his hammer and two drop cloths. After three quick whacks on the top edge of each window frame, the paint-splattered cloths were in position to block the views to the outside.

"Better?" he asked.

"Much better. Thanks," Gina said.

Her genuine smile caught him square in the gut. He found himself holding his breath until she turned away and looked back at Jacoby.

"How's that?" she asked. "And if you want to let the sun in during the day all you have to do is tie a scrap piece of fabric around the middle."

"Okay."

"Is there anything else?"

The boy opened his mouth, but snapped it shut again before he peeked over at Justin.

Okay, then.

He flipped the hammer in the air. Catching it easily by

the handle after it rotated a few times, he got a swift thrill when the kid's eyes grew wide. "I'll just put this back in my toolbox."

Gina's and Jacoby's heads were bent in a hushed conversation as he left the room. He returned a few minutes later, having no idea what they'd come up with next. Hopefully, a bedtime story and then lights out. Who knew getting a kid to sleep was such a big production?

He returned, happy the kid was lying down, tucked beneath the blankets with his bear. Their empty mugs sat on the small bedside table. He moved to the side of the bed where Gina sat.

Geez, he felt like a giant, towering over them. He dropped to a low crouch next to her. Big mistake. The move put him eye-level with her. She whirled to face him. Only a few inches separated them, and her signature scent filled his head, making him want to move even closer.

"Gina?"

The kid saying her name had both of them lurching apart. Justin fought against the instinct to physically shake off whatever spell she'd woven.

"So, are we all set?" he asked instead.

"Not quite," Gina said. "There's something else that needs to be taken care of."

"You've got another brilliant idea?"

"Well, I am gifted," she said, her smile a bit wobbly as she looked at him again. She paused and pulled in a shaky breath before she continued. "And you're the perfect man for the job."

"He is?"

"I am?"

Jacoby's and Justin's questions overlapped.

Gina nodded. "Yes, you are."

"Okay, what is it?"

"Monsters."

"Monsters?"

"You know, monsters and mutants, gremlins, goblins and googlebees."

Justin couldn't help himself, he smiled. "Googlebees?"

"Yes, googlebees, too." Gina shifted backward, putting more space between them as she tucked a long strand of hair behind one ear. "This room has probably been empty for years, which left plenty of time for all sorts of nasty ne'er-do-wells to move in. Your job is to tell them to leave. Right, Jacoby?"

Justin looked at the boy, who moved his head in a spirited nod.

"And just how am I supposed to do that?"

"You use that big, booming voice of yours I've heard so many times coming from the bar's kitchen…" Gina paused and he looked back at her again. "And you scare them away."

He waited for the punch line. Nothing. Both she and the kid continued to stare at him. Gina looking hopeful while Jacoby looked as if he expected Justin to refuse.

Resigned to making a fool of himself, he asked, "Do I just stand in the middle of the room and make a grand announcement?"

Both of them shook their heads.

"You need to go direct to their hiding place. Under the bed," Gina said.

"Under the bed?"

She pointed downward.

He sighed and dropped to his knees. Bending forward, he braced one hand on the floor and the other on the bed, right next to the warmth of Gina's hip.

Another mistake.

He pressed his fingers against the mattress, forcing them to lie flat instead of curving around the soft denim material of her jeans, and concentrated on the task at hand.

"All right, every monster, mutant, gremlin, goblin and googlebee, listen up! This room is now occupied and it's not big enough for all of you and the new tenant." He spoke in the best drill sergeant tone he could muster at the empty space beneath the bed. "It's time for the lot of you to pack your bags and hightail it out of town!"

He straightened, moved his hand away from Gina and centered his gaze on Jacoby. "Satisfied?"

The kid grinned. "That was totally awesome."

A rush of warmth filled him, and he immediately blamed it on his prone position seconds ago.

He turned to Gina. "Are you satisfied?"

"I agree, totally awesome."

Damn, now that warmth was centered in the middle of his chest and it burned. "So, can we turn out the lights and get some sleep?"

They both turned to Jacoby, who remained silent but his eyes darted across the room.

"Oh, of course," she said. "The closet."

"Huh?"

"Any self-respecting monster would head straight for the next closest hiding spot." She slanted her head toward the closed door on the opposite wall. "Then they wait until the coast is clear…"

"…and slip out from the crack beneath the door," Justin finished as her voice trailed off. "And go right on raising hel—ah, heck and making a general nuisance of themselves, right?"

"Wow," Jacoby whispered, pulling his teddy bear closer to his chest. "How did you know all that?"

"Because Justin was once a little boy, too." Gina tucked the blankets around the kid again. "He knows what you're feeling."

"What *I* feel is silly," Justin rasped as he got to his feet, bending close to Gina, his low words meant for her ears alone.

"You're doing fine," she whispered back.

Their eyes met and held for a long moment before Justin moved away. He walked to the closet door and took a deep breath. Yeah, he felt silly, but it was mixed with something else—something he couldn't put a name to, but it felt good and that was a feeling he hadn't experienced in a long time.

He yanked open the door and stood there, feet wide and hands on his hips. Hell, all he needed was a cape flapping in the breeze and a big red *S* on his chest.

"I thought I told you all to clear out and I meant it. There's no sense in trying to hide and don't bother thinking you can move to another nook, cranny or hiding spot anywhere in the cabin. You're not wanted here, so do like you were told. Pack your bags and get out of Destiny, every last one of you!"

He spun around, kicked the door shut with one boot heel and crossed his arms over his chest.

"Yeah!" Jacoby shouted with glee, and both he and Gina clapped.

Justin suddenly felt really stupid. He waved off their reaction and moved to the door, flipping the wall switch. The room went dark except for the glow from the night-light. "Okay, show's over. It's lights-out time."

Gina ruffled the boy's hair and rose from the bed. She started walking backward toward the door, keeping her eyes on Jacoby. Justin put out a hand to keep her from running into him, but she stopped just as his fingertips touched the softness of her sweater.

"Sweet dreams, Jacoby," she said gently.

"Okay," came the muffled reply.

Gina turned around and they nearly collided. She was so close he could feel the heat of her breath on his skin. Justin backed into the hallway. She followed.

"Gina, wait!"

The boy's cry had her turning back and Justin joined her in the doorway. She didn't reach for the light switch, so he didn't either.

"What is it?" she asked.

"Wh-what if they come back?"

"That's not going to happen. Your da—Justin did a great job of scaring all those crazy creatures off. I'm sure they are gone for good."

Justin ignored the quick twist in his gut as she almost called him a name he'd never thought would be his.

Dad.

She'd said it earlier, too, but she also must've picked up on the kid's unease and caught herself this time.

"But they might sneak back in after you leave," Jacoby continued his protest, "and after he goes to sleep, what's gonna stop 'em from coming back again?"

Back to square one.

Justin leaned in close to Gina and whispered in her ear. "Okay, Miss Gifted…you got another brilliant plan in that pretty little head of yours?"

He thought she was pretty.

Gina forced that reflection out of her head and concentrated on Jacoby's question.

She'd believed they'd done it; well, Justin had done most of the work. Thank goodness he'd been as sweet and understanding as her father had been to her all those years ago when the gremlins and googlebees invaded her bedroom when she was a little girl.

All she'd done was talk to Jacoby and get him to admit what was really bothering him. Justin had been the hero.

And he could be again.

She turned and waved her hand at his chest. "Strip."

Shock crossed his features. "Excuse me?"

"Your shirt, come on, take it off."

His expression turned wary, but his hands went up and behind his head and grabbed the back of his T-shirt. In one smooth motion, he pulled it off, baring a firm six pack, broad shoulders and muscular arms. And a Celtic knot armband tattoo encompassing his right beefy bicep.

The sight left her breathless.

"Now what?" he asked.

She took the shirt, the heat of his body still clinging to the fabric, and went back to Jacoby's side.

"I've got the perfect answer. Jacoby, honey, sit up." Her words came out a husky whisper and she hoped Justin didn't notice. "Here, let's put this on right over your pajamas."

The boy did as she asked, and she helped him tug the oversize shirt onto his small frame.

"Your…your dad and you look so much alike. If those bothersome beings even take one little peek in here, they'll see you in this shirt and think it's him sleeping here."

Jacoby ran his hands over the shirt that pooled at his waist. "Really?"

Gina knew she was taking a chance in addressing Justin as Jacoby's dad, but that's what he'd been tonight. He'd put aside his own feelings and done what his son had needed, from calling her for help to scaring away imaginary monsters.

"Really. And everyone knows those things can't see worth a darn in the dark. So even if they show up, which I seriously doubt, you will be well-protected. And I'm sure your dad doesn't mind you wearing his shirt."

Jacoby peeked around her to look at Justin. "Is it okay?"

"Yeah, sure. It looks great on you."

"Okay."

He flopped back down against his pillow and Gina again tucked him and his bear beneath the covers. This time his eyes were already closed and his breathing was slow and steady.

"'Night, Gina," he mumbled.

"Good night, sweetie." She brushed wisps of hair off his face, then stepped away from the bed.

"'Night, Dad."

Gina stilled for a moment before glancing at Justin. Did he hear the child's soft words? The stunned look on his face told her he had. With a quick "'Night," in return, he spun around and disappeared.

She checked on Jacoby again and found him fast asleep. Leaving the room, she paused to close the door, then went to find Justin. Back in the main room, Justin paced in the open area between the kitchen and living room. He'd pulled on a flannel shirt, but hadn't bothered with the buttons. Gina could feel uncertainty and doubt radiating off him.

"Why did he do that?" he asked in a low whisper.

She didn't pretend not to understand. "Because you're his father."

"We don't know that." He stopped and faced her, but then dropped his head back against the upper kitchen cabinets. Eyes closed, he thumped his head, each strike a punctuation mark to his words. "We. Don't. Know. That."

"Justin—"

"Even if I am that kid's father, I'm the worst possible person to take care of him." Eyes now open, but unfocused, he stared upward. "What the hell do I know about raising a kid?"

Gina's heart ached for him and the despair she heard in his voice. He had no idea how important what he'd done tonight—what he'd done the last two days—was to that sleeping little boy.

She moved closer, keenly aware of his nearness. "Jacoby's world…and yours was turned upside down two days ago. You've been doing a great job so far."

"I fed the kid and bought him some clothes, big deal." This time he did look at her, his words still a hushed whisper.

"That's not the same as being responsible for another person's life."

"It's part of it. Providing the basics is what a parent does."

"I'm not talking about that stuff. That was easy."

"Then why is Jacoby wearing brand-new pajamas with a full belly and sleeping in a bed for the first time in his life?" Gina gestured toward the room on the other side of the kitchen wall. "That's more than he's probably had in a long time."

"Anyone could have given him that stuff."

"But no one did, until you."

"I'm talking about more important things—"

"I know what you're talking about. How to be a good person, to know right from wrong, to work hard for what you want in life, to be nice—"

"And you think I'm the person who can teach him all that? So much for you being the smartest lady in town."

"You just need a little confidence in yourself."

He punched out a humorless laugh and looked away. "Sorry, fresh out of confidence."

Gina didn't pause to question what she was doing. She cupped his face, turning him to look at her. He returned her stare, almost silently daring her to do what she surely could read in her gaze.

In one motion, she rose to her tiptoes and placed her mouth to his. For a split second it was like kissing a statue, he held himself so still. Then his arms encircled her, his hands powerful as they stroked her back while his lips opened. The heat of his tongue had her readily parting to let him in. He pulled her hard against him, putting her curves flush with his solid, muscular body. Her hands went to the nape of his neck and she held on, sure the desire and passion in his kiss would cause her to splinter into a million pieces.

Oh, this man could kiss.

His hands tangled in her hair, then moved back to her waist where his fingers gathered the bottom edge of her sweater until he touched her skin, hot and needy.

And that's exactly how Justin made her feel. Hot and needy.

She'd fantasized about this moment for the last three months and the reality was a hundred times better than anything she'd imagined. And more.

He didn't just kiss with his mouth, but with his whole being.

He moved his hands away and she softly moaned at the loss, but then he trailed them over her jean-covered backside. Seconds later, he lifted her off her feet and carried her a few steps to place her on the counter that separated the kitchen from the living room.

He nudged her legs apart and stepped between them, his mouth never leaving hers. Arching her back, she strained to be closer, her hands moving to his upper arms, fisting the soft material of his shirt. He cradled the back of her head with one hand as he urged her to lean back into his hold. His other hand traced a path across her stomach before his fingertips slowly inched upward.

The need to breathe had her breaking free from his mouth, but the woodsy, masculine scent of his skin called to her and she buried her face into his neck.

She couldn't believe this was finally happening. Kissing Justin, being kissed by him, was just as wonderful as she'd dreamed it would be. The strength of his arms made her feel safe, the power in his kiss made her feel wanted.

And she wanted more.

"Justin…"

Seconds later, he scooted her off the counter and moved the two of them deeper into a dark corner of the shadowy kitchen. His mouth came down on hers again in a sizzling kiss until he suddenly broke free. They stood, with Gina pressed between the lower cabinets and his body. His breathing, short and fast and brushing over her ear, matched her own. His hands tightened for a moment before they dropped to right her clothing and he stepped back.

"What's going—"

He placed his fingers at her mouth. "I thought I heard—" A long moment passed before he dropped his hand. "I guess it was nothing. Look, we can't... We shouldn't be doing this."

"Why?"

Had she really said that aloud? Gina bit hard at her bottom lip, the innocence of her whispered question sounded so naive, so inexperienced even to her ears.

He took another step back but kept his voice low. "The list of reasons could take all night, but for starters, how about the fact our IQs are farther apart than Cheyenne and Miami?"

"This coming from a man who has the complete works of Shakespeare and volumes of poetry by Byron, Shelley and Keats on his bookshelf?"

"How do you know that?"

"Jacoby took me on a tour earlier, remember?"

"Speaking of Jacoby...reason number two. We aren't exactly alone here."

Shock washed over her as she realized the little boy might've walked in on them at any moment. No wonder Justin dragged her into the kitchen. "Oh, I didn't even think... I was so caught up in what we were doing...what you were..."

Her voice trailed off as a shaft of moonlight made it possible for Gina to look into Justin's eyes. For a moment there was something soft and pensive there, then he blinked and she saw nothing but emptiness.

She jerked out of his arms. Grabbing her purse and coat, she started for the front door. "I should go."

"Gina, this...this isn't going to happen again." He started to follow her, then stopped. "It can't happen again."

But she wanted it to. She wanted to kiss him again with every fiber of her being and she could've sworn he'd wanted it, too.

"Well, I guess we'll have to keep that in mind if we ever find ourselves alone in the dark again."

Chapter Seven

One week. Seven days. One hundred and sixty-eight hours. Ten thousand and eighty minutes since he'd seen the woman who'd given him one damn fine, soul-stirring, libido-reviving kiss.

Yeah, Justin had just figured that out in his head.

Not that his mental calculations helped in his struggle to keep his mind on his job as he prepped for the dinner crowd at The Blue Creek Saloon.

He was also trying—unsuccessfully—to forget what he'd said to Gina after forcing himself to pull away from her mouth, her touch and out of her arms.

And it wasn't because of the way his body responded to the first woman he'd held in his arms in three long months. It was because she was the one woman he couldn't have.

The fact she'd left for a week in the Caribbean with her girlfriends the next day wasn't helping. It should. That whole "out of sight, out of mind" thing, but it wasn't.

He'd hurt her.

He'd seen it in her eyes when she'd looked at him, heard it in her voice. But it was for the best. She'd been laying on the daddy hero worship a bit too thick and when she'd touched him, turned his head to face her, he'd thought he'd telegraphed the message "back off" loud and clear.

Apparently she'd read his stare differently.

And before they'd ended up in a tangle of clothes and quilts in front of his fireplace, he'd had to do something, say something, to knock that starry-eyed look off her face. Just like he'd done that afternoon after she'd stepped forward and provided an alibi for him when the sheriff thought Justin was somehow responsible for the fire that destroyed the Dillon family home.

Didn't she get it?

He was one hundred percent the wrong guy for her. Ex-con, from the wrong side of the tracks, nothing but trouble… all the clichés fit him perfectly, but Gina was too innocent, too nice to see Justin for what he really was.

He put the prepared vegetables for tonight's salads back into the walk-in refrigerator and took out the fresh hamburger for the mini burgers. Instead of letting his thoughts stray to memories of warm skin and soft lips while he mindlessly molded perfectly formed patties, he thought about all that happened over the last week.

He'd settled Jacoby in at school and the boy's doctor's appointment had gone okay. Gage had called and said he'd found a Mazie Smith living in Templeton, Colorado, but other than learning that Zoe and Jacoby had stayed with her for a few months, and lifted the woman's stash of emergency cash on their way out, there was still no clue of Zoe's whereabouts. On a better note, the other two cooks had agreed to shift the kitchen staff hours around, so now Justin worked days and had his nights free.

For a seven-year-old.

That was also when he'd looked at the week's schedule and

seen Gina's block of hours with a red line running through it. It hadn't taken long for Ric Murphy, who seemed to have appointed himself Gina's personal guard dog, to let Justin know she'd grabbed a last-minute cancellation and joined Barbie Felton, and probably a thousand other college kids, at a beach resort on a tropical island.

Justin had never experienced spring break, but he'd seen enough of those videos and reality shows to know all the craziness that went on. He'd found himself more than once wondering if Gina had finally found that inner wild child she'd been hunting for since coming back to town.

Had she joined in on any of those extreme contests that usually involved more alcohol than common sense? Had some muscle-bound college kid helped her to cut loose?

"Hey, aren't those supposed to have a bit of heft to them?"

Surprised, Justin looked up to find Barbie leaning against the large counter where he worked.

They were back.

Barbie wore the usual outfit of a Blue Creek waitress, a tight T-shirt with the bar's logo, a short jean shirt and cowboy boots. All designed to show off miles of skin, newly tanned in Barbie's case.

He half expected Gina to walk through the swinging doors next, dressed the same way.

Mad at himself for the hot flare that shot through him at the idea of finally seeing Gina again, he returned his attention to the hamburger in his hand. It was flatter than a pancake. He folded the meat back into his palm and started over.

"Want to share what's making you pound that meat into submission?" Barbie asked.

Yeah, like that was going to happen. "No."

"You know, you've got yourself a cute little boy." She ran a finger along the edge of the tray where the finished patties lay. "He's got your eyes. I noticed that right off when Gina showed me a picture of him and Jack—"

He cut her off. "Gina has a picture of Jacoby?"

Barbie's hand stilled, but her mouth rose in a smile. "Yeah, on her cell phone. She got a text message a few days ago while we were rocking the beach in our teenie-weenie bikinis."

Justin tried not to picture Gina in a 'teenie-weenie' anything while figuring out who would've sent her a picture.

The answer came to him right away.

Racy.

He and Jacoby had eaten at her and Gage's house last week. He'd gotten the third degree from both of them after Jacoby had shared the story of chasing away monsters, including Gina's part in the evening's events. Later that same night, his sister had asked him if he knew why Gina had suddenly requested a week's vacation the very next day.

He'd told her he had no idea, which was the truth, in a manner of speaking.

"Hey, Dillon." Ric Murphy walked into the kitchen. "Your sister is looking for you."

Justin shook his head at the guy's ongoing crappy attitude toward him. The last time he'd actually looked happy was months ago when Justin made it clear he had no interest in Gina.

No interest? Yeah, right.

Ric's scowl turned to a smile when he spotted Barbie. "Hey, the beach girls are back. I wish I'd gone with you all."

Barbie turned on the charm. "You should've!"

"Yeah, well, the log mansion that Murphy Mountain Homes is putting together on the old Harris land needed extra hands and my brothers expected me to pitch in, no questions asked."

"Oh, did you find out who's building that place?"

Ric shook his head. "Nope, my brother Bryant would only say it's a privately held company. So, how was your trip?"

"Boys, booze and beaches." The leggy waitress replied with a grin. "It was awesome."

Awesome, huh?

Barbie's description of their trip swirled inside Justin's head as he exited through the swinging doors and headed toward his sister's office. He found her on the phone. She waved him in and kept talking.

Jack rose from the couch and bounced over to greet him. After allowing Justin to scratch him behind his ears, the dog started pacing between him and the door Justin had closed behind him.

"What's he doing?" He asked after Racy ended her call.

"He's probably looking for Jacoby," she said, snapping her cell phone closed. "He's really attached to the kid."

"Yeah, so much so he figured out how to take a picture of the two of them and send it via a text message all the way to the Caribbean."

A smile took over her features. "You know about that."

Justin dropped into one corner of the leather couch and Jack climbed up next to him. "Whatever gave you the idea to send Gina that picture?"

"Because Jacoby asked me to."

That surprised him. "He did? Why?"

"We were doing the dishes while you and Gage were enjoying some man-time downstairs playing pool." She leaned forward in her chair. "He said he was worried she might forget him while she was gone."

Justin had no idea the boy felt that way.

When Jacoby had asked about her, Justin had told him she'd gone on vacation. He'd thought that was the end of it because Jacoby hadn't mentioned her again. What did it mean that neither one of them seemed to be able to get Gina out of their heads?

"Hey, you still with me?"

Mentally shaking off his thoughts of Gina, Justin tried to read the worried expression in his sister's eyes.

Something was going on.

"I asked for you because Leeann is on her way," Racy continued when he remained silent. "To speak with you."

Deputy Leeann Harris.

Justin had known her as one of his sister's best friends growing up and as the girl who'd entered tons of beauty pageants. It seemed she'd always been in the newspaper as Miss something or other. The last he'd heard Leeann had left town to become a famous model. She'd been a popular choice of wall art on the concrete walls in his former home. He had been surprised when he returned home to find her working for the sheriff's department.

Now she was assigned to the search for Jacoby's mother.

The news that the deputy was on her way had him sitting up straight. "Why? What's going on?"

Racy shrugged. "I don't know. She called earlier and asked if you were working today. She said she tried to call you directly, but you weren't answering."

"I forgot my phone at home," he answered. Did the sheriff's department have something on Zoe? Maybe even found her? "Jacoby didn't want to get out of bed, and then he put up a stink about taking a shower. It went downhill from there."

"How did his doctor's visit go?"

Justin knew what his sister was doing and he let her distract him from thinking about Zoe. "It went okay. Jacoby's fine physically, even though he's a bit undersize for his age. Another ten pounds couldn't hurt, but at least his immunizations are now up to date."

"And you did the DNA testing?"

So much for distraction. Justin nodded.

"Do the results really matter to you?"

A ripple of trepidation sliced through his gut. "I'm ninety

percent sure he's my son, but if not…well, I wouldn't want some other father out there not knowing the boy exists."

"That's not going to matter if you can't find his mother."

Maybe the sheriff's department already had. "I know. Jacoby is my responsibility…for now."

"And when the results come back that you're a match?"

"Then I'm a dad."

A name Jacoby had been calling him for a week now.

It'd started the morning after the monster exorcism, when the kid walked into the kitchen asking for breakfast, still wearing Justin's T-shirt. It seemed as if he made sure to include the word every time he spoke. Justin had asked why a few days later, Jacoby simply stated *dad* was a word he'd never had the chance to use before, and damn, if Justin wasn't getting used to—

A knock rapped on the door.

"Come on in," Racy called out.

Leeann entered. "Hi, there, I see you found him."

Leeann was a striking woman, even wearing the standard khaki uniform of the sheriff's department and her former waist-length hair now cut short.

Noticing the deputy's hair instantly made him think of that pink streak in Gina's. *Congratulations, Dillon. You managed to go a half hour without thinking about the woman.*

"Hello, Justin."

Leeann's voice cut into his thoughts. It still carried that ice-running-through-her-veins tone he remembered from years ago. Or was that money? Thanks to her inheritance, the sale of the land where her former childhood home once stood and her modeling career, he'd bet she had plenty of money stashed away.

He wondered again why she was working as a public servant. "Deputy Harris."

Racy walked around her desk. "I'll give you two some privacy."

"You don't have to go," Justin said. "You know I'll just tell you everything later."

His sister's smile spoke to how their relationship had changed over the last few months. "Thanks, but if I know Lee, she's going to want to do this by the book, and that means just the two of you."

Leeann nodded in agreement and waited until Racy left before she crossed the room. She sat in a chair opposite him, pausing a moment to offer a hello to the dog.

Justin leaned forward. "Did you find Zoe?"

"We're not sure." She pulled out a small black notebook and flipped a few pages. "Did you ever know Zoe Ellis by any other name?"

"The weekend we spent together, she told me her name was Susie." Justin realized he'd never relayed that information to the sheriff's office. "I confronted her about that when she was here. She admitted she lied. Said her real name was Zoe Ellis."

"A car matching the vague description Jacoby provided was found abandoned in Reno—"

Justin sprang to the edge of the sofa. "Reno!"

Leeann held up a hand to silence him and kept talking. "A child's drawing was found in the backseat. It was signed 'Jacoby Ellis.'"

Justin closed his eyes for a moment, but opened them when Leeann continued.

"I sent a copy of that old photograph of you and Miss Ellis to my contact at the Washoe County sheriff's office. She took it to local businesses near where the car was found. A second-rate casino came up with a possible match, but said the woman called herself Susie Ellsworth."

His heart dropped to his feet. "Did they find her?"

Leeann shook her head. "The people at the casino said she told them a sob story about running from an abusive husband and didn't want to fill out any paperwork. She worked as a cocktail waitress for a few days—all wages under the table—and then took off with a high roller throwing around a lot of money."

This was unbelievable. Justin dropped his head and gripped his fingers, his knuckles turning white from the pressure.

"You okay?"

Leeann's soft voice surprised him. He released a pent-up breath he hadn't even realized he was holding and forced his hands to relax. "Yeah, so what do we do now?"

She shut her notebook and met his gaze. "We keep looking, under both names, for her. Have you had the DNA test done you mentioned last week?"

Justin nodded. "I should have the results in a few days."

"Good. The sooner paternity is established the better it will be, for you and that little boy." Leeann rose from her seat. "We'll be keeping an eye out for Zoe and her friend, if they are still together, as well."

"You think she might just show back up here?"

"If she thinks she's found someone to support her…"

Leeann's voice trailed off, leaving unsaid the suggestion that Jacoby's mother could snatch the boy away as easily as she left him behind.

Justin stood, too, the urge to pick up Jacoby from the after-school program suddenly very powerful. "Fine."

The deputy looked at him for a long moment and Justin returned her stare. She'd done the same thing last week at the sheriff's office when Gage filled her in on the details of the case. He didn't know if she was testing him, but he held her gaze until she broke free and turned toward the door.

"For what it's worth—"

His words stopped her. Words he hadn't even planned to say, but now that he'd started, he kept talking. "I appreciate your hard work on this. Considering our somewhat tainted history, you could've—"

Leeann spun around to face him, her voice low. "I'm just doing my job."

"Well, thanks anyway."

Leeann nodded and left the office. Waiting a few minutes to give her a head start, Justin followed and ran into his sister in the hallway.

"So, how did it go with you and Leeann?"

"Ah, I'll talk to you later, okay?" He looked at his watch. "I need to get to the school and pick up Jacoby."

After a quick hug goodbye, Justin headed out to the parking lot. Even though he was running late, he stuck to the speed limit, despite the threat Leeann alluded to in this ongoing mess about Zoe Ellis or Susie Ellsworth or whatever her name was.

Minutes later, he parked outside the school. He got out of his truck and took a deep, cleansing breath. It was cool now that the sun had gone down, and he was anxious to find Jacoby in the crowd. Then he saw him racing toward him, his tattered pillowcase bouncing off one shoulder and papers in his hand.

Justin knelt as the boy careened into him. "Hey, slow down, buddy."

"Dad! Dad! Guess what?" Jacoby jumped around with little-boy excitement. "Gina's back in town!"

Was it less than an hour ago Justin had found out the same thing? "How do you know that?"

"Look at this!" Jacoby shoved a piece of paper in Justin's face. "She's doing a story hour at the town library. Tonight! Can we go? Huh? Huh? Can we?"

Chapter Eight

The familiar scent of clean male skin mixed with a hint of garlic and pine trees tickled Gina's nose. It nudged out the sweet and sweaty smells of crayons and candy drifting up from the children sitting at her feet.

Justin was close by.

She could actually feel his presence. As romance-booky as that sounded. Of course, at last count, she'd consumed eight romance novels during her week in paradise and had an unfinished one tucked in her purse.

Once she, Barbie, Jeannie and Tina had settled into their seats on the plane, she'd pulled out an unfinished biography of one of her favorite English poets, but Barbie had snatched it out of her hands.

"Absolutely not," her friend declared. "If you are going to read this week—and I'm sure you will—it's only flirty and frisky novels for you!"

She'd then handed her a paperback with a man on the cover, headless but showing wide shoulders, a perfect set of six-pack abs and wearing nothing but a pair of faded jeans that hugged him in all the right places.

Gina had immediately thought of Justin. Not good, considering getting away from him was the reason for her impromptu vacation.

The same night she'd raced out of Justin's cabin after that heartbreaking kiss, Barbie had called offering her the last-minute vacancy on a trip to the islands. She'd jumped at the chance to put a few thousand miles between her and the sexy coworker-slash-new-father whose kisses were a hundred times better than anything she'd read over the last week.

Forcing her attention back to the open children's book on her lap, Gina managed to get through the rest of the words on the page, despite the lower and huskier tone of her voice.

Her gaze scanned the kids in the children's area as she turned the page, making eye contact with Jacoby in the back row. He gave a discreet wave. She winked in return. Behind him were a group of jean-clad legs, visible from the knees down, and a variety of work boots, sandals and cowboy boots.

So which of those legs belonged to Justin?

He wouldn't just leave the little boy alone in the library, would he? Then again, maybe Justin wasn't the one who'd brought Jacoby, which blew her "he's close by" theory out of the water.

Maybe it was all in her head.

And her heart.

Gina steered her focus to the book again, losing herself in the story. The inflections she used in her voice added a bit of flair and drama to the words and the children sat forward, their faces reflecting delight at her theatrical approach.

She'd been surprised when her mother told her just last night as she got back from vacation that she'd volunteered Gina to take over the library's story hour. But the girl who normally read to the kids needed emergency surgery, so Gina agreed.

After she finished, everyone clapped and then stood to pull on their jackets. She spoke with a few kids and their parents, but her gaze continued to snag on Jacoby standing off to one side by himself, his tattered pillowcase clutched in one hand.

Once alone, she waved him over and dropped to a crouch in front of him so they were eye to eye. "Hey, I'm glad to see you here."

"Wow, you're so brown."

Despite daily lathering of sunscreen, Gina was sporting a brown glow thanks to a touch of Native American heritage in the Steele family bloodline. "I just got back from vacation. Spent a lot of time on the beach and swimming in the ocean."

"Cool! I've never seen the ocean, except on television."

"Well, it's even more beautiful in person. All shades of blue and green, from the lightest aqua to deepest navy. And warm enough you can bathe in it."

Jacoby giggled. "Gee, that's not like our lake. The water is supposed to be blue, too, but it looks black to me and it's cold. We worked on the dock yesterday and my dad said I could put my toes in the water. Brrrrr!"

A flutter crossed Gina's heart at hearing Jacoby call Justin by that special title. *Don't ask, don't ask, don't—* "So, where's your dad now?" *So much for willpower.*

"He's in the truck."

Gina frowned. "You're alone? Why would your dad send you in here by yourself?"

"He didn't."

Jacoby had opened his mouth, but the words, low and deep, came from overhead.

From a pair of battle-worn work boots planted right behind the little boy, Gina allowed her gaze to travel upward over faded denim, a worn leather belt and a black T-shirt partially visible beneath a threadbare jean jacket. Rising slowly, she continued her perusal over broad shoulders and a day's worth of stubble that only seemed to harden angular cheeks and jaw. She reached dark eyes staring at her from beneath the frayed rim of a baseball cap that had seen better days.

"Justin." Darn, her voice still held that husky tone. "Hello."

His gaze slowly trailed the length of her before zeroing in on her mouth for a full second. Then he looked into her eyes. "Hello yourself."

"Did you get it, Dad? Did ya?"

Justin handed whatever it was he carried to the boy. "Right where you left it on the front seat."

Jacoby took the paper and tugged on Gina's hand at the same time. "Look! I drew this!"

It took a hard blink to break the hold of Justin's gaze on her. She again dropped to her knees, this time to look at a crayon drawing. Two figures with matching dark hair stood in a kitchen while a fire blazed in the nearby fireplace. "Wow, this must be of the two of you, huh?"

Jacoby beamed. "We're baking cookies. We did it twice this week, peanut butter and snickerdoodles. Those are my favorites."

"And what's this?" Gina pointed to an oversize box near the fireplace.

"That's our new television. Dad and I love to watch the vinege cartoons together."

"Vintage." Justin offered the correct word.

"Vintage," Jacoby repeated, then leaned in closer and dropped his voice to a whisper. "That means old."

She smiled. "Which old cartoons are your favorites?"

"I like *Tom & Jerry*. Dad likes the *Justice League*. He says Wonder Woman is his favorite."

That caused Gina to look up at Justin. "Wonder Woman?"

He offered a casual shrug. "What can I say? I'm a sucker for a woman in a strapless one-piece."

How about a strapless bikini?

The silent question echoed in Gina's head as she thought about the skimpy bathing suit—purchased on a whim—she'd been wearing just over twenty-four hours ago.

Happy that she'd managed not to ask the question aloud, Gina turned her attention back to Jacoby. "Well, that's a terrific picture. You did a great job."

"It's for you." Jacoby thrust the paper into her hands.

"Me? Are you sure you don't want to give it to your dad?"

"Naw, he's already got lots of my drawings hanging on the fridge and stuff. He says I'm a regular P-Pablo Picasso. He's a famous painter, you know. Besides, I signed it to you." Jacoby pointed at the writing in the corner. "See? Right there."

She did see. In shaky block letters it read: TO GINA. LOVE, JACOBY.

A sudden lump in her throat kept her from answering, but she nodded her thanks. Just then, a red-headed boy called Jacoby over to see something.

"That's Dustin. Can I go?" Jacoby asked.

Gina stood, her eyes glued to the paper, but saw Justin hesitate for a moment before giving the boy a quick nod. She turned and laid the drawing on a nearby waist-high bookshelf, smoothing the creased corners with her fingertips.

"He worked really hard on that."

She whirled around. Justin had moved in behind her, trapping her in a corner. "I can tell. It's beautiful and I'll treasure it."

Something hot flared in his eyes, darkening them. He started to take another step toward her, then shoved his hands deep into his pockets and inched backward instead. "I need to talk to you."

It was noisy in the children's section, so Gina took a step closer to hear him. "Ah, okay."

"Can we go somewhere so I don't sound like an idiot?"

His whispered voice was far from idiotic. Heck, his soft tone was turning her insides to mush just like that night in his kitchen. And where had that led? To her feeling like a fool for the second time in a matter of days.

Kissing Justin had been the last thing on her mind when he'd called asking for help and yet they'd ended up in each other's arms. Thanks to her. She'd kissed him first. Of course, he'd quickly taken over, literally sweeping her off her feet. Who knew where it would've led—

"Gina?"

Her face flamed at being caught in the memory and at the desperate need to repeat that mistake, right here and now.

Hoping her tan hid the evidence of her embarrassment, she grabbed her jacket and purse, noticing the number of fascinated glances from the other parents. "I—I need to get to work. It's my first night back since—"

"Your sudden vacation. Yeah, I know. Come on, I'll walk you to your car." Justin held out Jacoby's picture to her, his voice at a normal level as he turned toward his son. "Come on, bud. We're out of here."

Jacoby raced over to them. "Dad, did you hear? A famous race car driver from right here in Destiny was in a real bad car accident!"

Jacoby's friend and the older man with him, obviously his father from the matching strawberry-blond hair and freckles, joined them. "He's talking about Bobby Winslow," the man said. "One of the other parents just heard it on the radio. I guess he crashed while getting ready for an upcoming race."

The sound of a whispered curse had Gina looking at Justin, the strong line of his jaw clenched tight, concern etched on his face. "Are you okay?"

He glanced at her, then tugged his cap a bit farther down on his forehead. "I'm fine. Is he hurt bad?"

The man shrugged, waving to someone who called his name. "All the report said was that he's in critical condition. I'm guessing they'll have more about it on television tonight. I've got to run."

The murmuring of the crowd grew louder as the news of the accident spread. Gina didn't know Bobby Winslow personally, but he'd graduated from high school with Gage and was a local hero to many in the town. "That is just terrible. I hope he's going to be all right."

"Yeah," Justin paused and swallowed hard as he motioned for Gina toward the rear entrance of the library. "Me, too."

"Did you know him, Dad?" Jacoby tugged on Justin's jacket as he walked between the two of them. "The guy in the accident?"

They reached the back door and Justin held it open for everyone to walk through. "Bobby and I are—were friends, a long time ago. At least we were until he and Leann Harris started dating. We haven't kept in touch since he left to go into the army, but I've followed his career. Kind of nice to know the kid who used to race along Destiny's mountain roads made good."

They headed across the parking lot, dusk closing in fast. Gina shivered in the night's chill, but maybe it was because Justin's hand, warm and firm against her lower back, guided her.

Jacoby raced ahead to Justin's truck parked beside her car at the far end of the lot. Their driver's side doors were next to each other as she'd backed into the space when she'd arrived.

When they reached the vehicles, Justin dropped his hand to unlock his truck and open the door. "Come on, Jacoby, jump in."

Jacoby lifted one foot to climb in, but then spun back around. "Oh, Gina, I forgot to tell you! I'm a Beaver!"

Gina smiled, not sure what the boy meant. "You are?"

"Yep, I'm playing baseball. Actually, it's T-ball, but after a couple of years I can move up to a Little League team."

"That's wonderful. What position do you play?"

"Left field. It's kinda boring 'cause most kids can't hit the ball that far, but it's still fun. Will you come see me play sometime?"

"Of course."

Jacoby gave her a big smile and then climbed in the truck.

"What are the rules?" Justin asked him.

"Put my seatbelt on and don't touch anything on your side."

Justin nodded and started to close the door, when Jacoby popped back into view. "Hey, did you get the picture of me and Jack while you were on your trip?"

"Yes, I did." Gina pulled out her cell phone and brought up the image. She stepped closer, wedging in between Justin and his truck to show it to the boy. "Thanks for sending it."

"Cool!"

She stepped back again so Justin could close the door, tucking her phone in her purse, her keys already in her hand. She had no idea what he wanted to talk to her about, but her instincts told her it had something to do with those few minutes they'd spent in his darkened kitchen last week and how his simple request for help had turned into—

"Oh, hey, Dad?"

Justin yanked the ball cap off his head. He rubbed his forehead with the back of his hand in obvious frustration and braced one arm on the open truck door. "Yes?"

"I had a friend named Bobby. He was hurt in a car accident, too. I don't know if he's okay now 'cause we moved, but my teacher told me he would be." Jacoby sniffed and wiped at his nose with his sleeve. "Anyway, I'm sorry your friend got hurt."

The surprise on Justin's face and the sincerity of Jacoby's words had Gina blinking back the sting of tears. The newly formed bond between these two was so clearly visible that she almost felt like an outsider.

"Thanks, buddy." Justin reached out and put his cap on the boy's head. "Now, scoot in and get your seat belt on."

Jacoby pushed the bill of the cap upward from where it'd fallen over his eyes and grinned. "Roger."

Justin closed the truck door with a soft click and stood there, his hands pressed against the glass.

"You two have come really far over the last week."

"Not as far as you think." He didn't look at her as he spoke. "For all the cookie baking and cartoon watching, there've been a few times when he's woken up screaming from nightmares he can't…or won't talk about."

"Oh, Justin, I'm so sorry." She couldn't stop herself from touching him. Gripping tightly to his jacket with one hand, she laid the other on his wrist, feeling the leashed power of his constricted muscles. "I don't know what I can do, but I'll gladly listen if you want to talk."

He pulled from her touch and dropped his hands. He then tried to step back deeper into the shadows, but a large tree at the edge of the parking lot blocked his path. "That's not what I wanted—not why I asked you to come out here."

Gina gripped her keys tight, fighting to maintain a casual air despite the tension that hung heavy between them. "Okay, then, what was it? I'm going to be late for work."

"I owe you an apology."

His simple words surprised her. He wanted to apologize? For what?

Oh, no, was he going to say he was sorry about kissing her?

"I've been really hard on you, more than I should have, in light of all you've done since Jacoby showed up." He tunneled his fingers through his hair, his gaze focused on the night sky. "Right from the start you've been great and I've been behaving like a horse's ass—"

"I already accepted one apology from you in the diner. I think that's enough." Gina needed to stop this right here and now. He was working his way up to something and she couldn't stand to hear him say he was sorry about that kiss. "You needed help, so I helped."

"You came over to the cabin that night when you could've—hell, should've hung up on me." He kept talking, pausing to gesture toward the truck before his hand fell to his side. "You easily figured out what was keeping Jacoby from going to bed and how did I show my thanks? By doing the one thing I promised myself I'd never—"

"Like I said, it's no big deal."

Get in the car. Now.

The words flashed inside Gina's head and she shouldered past him. It took two tries but she managed to get her key into the lock without crushing the rolled picture from Jacoby.

"I—I would've done the same for anyone," she sputtered. "And don't think twice about that kiss. It was no big deal."

Silence filled the air before he spoke. "No big deal?"

He echoed her words in a low tone that warmed her neck. He must've moved in behind her. If she leaned back the slightest bit…

She twisted the key, popped the lock and yanked her door open. "Yes, just a spur-of-the-moment thing. It'd been a long weekend, you were exhausted and I caught you off guard." She was babbling, which was better than letting him talk, so she kept at it as she wiggled into the driver's seat.

"It was just a friendly kiss between two consenting adults. We can do that, you know? Be friends? So, let it go. Okay?"

* * *

Friends?

Justin watched the taillights of Gina's car fade in the distance as he stood next to his idling truck.

What the hell just happened?

When Jacoby first asked to come to the library's story hour specifically to see Gina, Justin had tried to talk him out of it. Not even a burger and fries from Sherry's Diner had been enough to change the kid's mind. Finally admitting he wanted to see Gina as much as Jacoby did, he'd relented and they arrived after the story hour had already started. The sight of her bright blue eyes, brown curls still sporting that vivid pink band and her golden tanned skin had him mesmerized.

He'd watched her smile, listened to the natural huskiness of her voice as she'd told the story and even with his head still in a fog over all Leeann had told him earlier, he was more determined than ever to give Gina the apology she deserved.

The apology he should've given her in his darkened kitchen after he'd managed to do the last thing in the world he'd wanted and pulled away from her.

So, how had their conversation gone from his trying to say he was sorry to her declaring they were friends? And the kiss she'd laid on him was no big deal? What did that mean? She would've done that for anyone?

He doubted she meant it the way it sounded, but it bugged him all the same. It'd been easy to tell she didn't have a lot of experience in the kissing department, but what she lacked in style, she more than made up for with untapped passion.

A passion that almost drove him to do the stupidest thing in his life.

Hope.

Hope that she'd meant it when she crawled into his arms, sighed into his mouth and wrapped that sweet body around him. Hope that she might care for the boy who seemed to have too few people concerned about him in his young life. Hope that maybe he, too, could have the same things in life that other people took for granted.

Friends?

Damn, he was really in trouble now.

Justin turned, but when his hand landed on the truck's door handle, he knew he wasn't alone. Widening his stance, he quickly pivoted back again.

"I think it's a disgrace," a woman said, staring at him.

Justin guessed that she and the man with her were in their midfifties. He didn't think he knew them, but something was familiar. "Pardon me?"

"There is no excuse for you." The woman, dressed in a long overcoat and sensible shoes, her hair pulled back off her face, continued. "We don't think you're a proper guardian for that young boy."

Justin was dumbfounded. "Is that right?"

"That's right." The man beside her spoke up, the Stetson pulled low over his eyes making it impossible to see his face. "Believe me, child services is watching you. You're too much like your old man and your brother to be any good for that kid. The last thing we need is someone raising another Dillon to cause nothing but trouble."

"And just because your sister managed to hook up with the good sheriff doesn't mean you've earned the right to be here." The woman tugged on the man's arm. "We don't want your kind in our town. Come on, Harold. Let's go."

Shock turned to anger, rushing to life in a black fury that boiled in his veins. A veiled voice of caution struggled to overcome his rage. When it reached him it sounded sweet and soothing.

It sounded like Gina.

He pressed his boots to the concrete, successfully fighting the urge to race after the couple and show them just what he thought of their advice. Intense gratitude filled him that the rolled-up windows kept Jacoby from hearing the couple's words as Justin watched the two of them walk away.

It wasn't until they disappeared into the darkness that he realized his hands were clenched in tight fists. He shook them loose, took a deep breath and tried to put their words out of his head as he climbed into the truck. But deep inside, he knew what they'd said had been the truth.

Chapter Nine

"Gina, please, we need you! You have to help us!"

Trying to ignore her sister's whining was like trying to ignore fingernails being dragged across a chalkboard.

Impossible.

"Look, I agreed to come with you and Mom to help pick out a dress." Gina leaned her head back, raising her voice to be heard over the dressing room door. "Which you waited until the last possible minute to shop for, I might add. But I am not, repeat, *not* interested in playing chaperone."

"But this isn't just any dance. It's the spring formal, the last dance we seniors have before graduation. If we don't get enough chaperones, the school might cancel it." Giselle's muffled reply came through the door. "We're celebrating the founding of the high school back in the fifties. The whole theme is based on that decade."

This is why they were spending Saturday night sifting through racks of dresses, both authentic and reproductions, in Cheyenne's finest vintage clothing store.

"Fine, it's a big deal," Gina conceded, "but that doesn't mean I'm going to—"

The chime from her cell phone announced an incoming text message, cutting her off. She dug into her pocket, admonishing her heart for the now-familiar quickening that had become common over the last week.

It wasn't Justin. She hadn't even looked yet, but she knew it wasn't him. Not hard to come to that conclusion as she'd hardly spoken to the man since Monday night in the library parking lot. The few times she'd seen him at work and offered a hello resulted in a mumbled reply and nothing more. She'd seen Jacoby during story hour at the library, but it had been Racy who had brought him both times.

Friends? Yeah, right. Justin was plainly not interested in a friendship, much less anything else, with her. She flipped open her phone and read the message.

Don't be a nudge and leave us with only old people as guards. Come to the dance.

Garrett.

Giselle's twin obviously wasn't planning on majoring in English at Duke University in the fall.

"Stop trying to double-team me," she said to Giselle as she typed the same words to her brother. "I'm not interested."

"But you'd have a good time." Giselle cracked open the dressing room door and peeked out. "And if anyone needs a good time, it's you."

Gina twisted in her chair to look at her sister. "What does that mean?"

"You've been acting like a slug ever since you got back from your trip. Other than being kid happy over reading Dr. Seuss to a bunch of rug rats, that is."

"Hey!"

"Giselle, leave your sister alone." Sandy Steele came back into the changing area, her arms loaded down with dresses in a rainbow of pastel colors. "If she doesn't want to go, I'm sure she has a good reason."

"Thanks, Mom." Gina's eye caught the glittering black at the bottom of the pile.

"Of course, you never did attend a formal dance of your own." Sandy added the dresses to a holding rack, except for a lemony-yellow chiffon number Giselle was already reaching for. "I always considered that a shame. Perhaps you could get dressed up and attend this event."

Gina groaned as her sister giggled and disappeared back into her dressing room. "Mom, not you, too."

"I think you'd have a wonderful time." Her mother turned to her and held out a black, strapless dress with a fitted bodice and a voluminous skirt of starched netting that glistened under the dressing room lights.

"At a high school dance?"

"You're not so far removed from high school, dear."

Gina couldn't keep from gently touching the dress. Three layers of tulle made up the skirt, the top layer lightly dusted with silver glitter, the middle black and ruffled and the bottom a deep chocolate. Gorgeous. "I'll be twenty-three in a few months."

"The perfect age to keep an eye on a group of teenagers while still having good time," Sandy said, then whispered, "Why don't you at least try it on?"

"Oh, I'm not dressed to try on anything formal."

"It's more about undressing than dressing, sis," Giselle called out. "Mom, I need some help in here."

"The bodice is boned, and the crinoline petticoats are already sewn into the skirt." Her mother pushed the hanger at Gina. "You don't need to wear anything special underneath."

She took the dress, surprised at its substantial weight. "I don't know…"

"It can't hurt to try it on." Her mother turned Gina toward

an empty dressing room. "As soon as I saw it, I thought of you."

Stepping inside the room, Gina hung the dress on the closest hook and stripped down to her panties before she could change her mind. She undid the side zipper, stepped into the dress and slid it into place while keeping her back to the room's mirror.

It took some work to get the zipper back up, but she did it. Then she noticed her socks. Nope, they had to go, too. She toed them off, noting she needed to get to Ursula's for another pedicure, and turned to face the mirror.

Her eyes widened.

Wow.

Gina inched toward her image, amazed at how the heart-shaped bodice hugged her breasts and the fitted structure did wonders for her posture. Her tanned skin glowed. Perching on tiptoes told her high heels were a necessity.

So was an updo hairstyle. She pulled a hair clip from her purse and seconds later her riot of curls was off her shoulders. They were still a mess, but it worked for now. She twirled back and forth, loving the swishing noise the tulle made.

Definitely a *wow* kind of dress.

Could she do this? Chaperone a high school dance?

It would be fun to see her siblings and their friends all dressed up and while a few teachers had been invited, the dance committee, of which Giselle was in charge, needed to secure the rest of the chaperones. Parents had quickly been scratched off the list, for obvious reasons according to Giselle, but older siblings would be perfect. Except if the older sibling was the town sheriff or his wife. That let Gage and Racy off the hook.

Okay, so now they had her thinking about it.

But she couldn't show up alone. Talk about the heights of geekiness. Who could she ask—

No, no, no.

Gina's cell phone chimed again and she jumped at the chance to end the ridiculous thought running through her head. She flipped it open and read the text message.

Go to the freaking dance.

Barbie. Geez, her sister was now getting Gina's friends involved.

Would you like to go to a high school dance? she typed in response.

A minute later came Barbie's reply. *Been there, done that. If you're looking for a date, try a guy. Then there's no question about who leads who when dancing.*

Gina rolled her eyes. Another message immediately followed.

Ask Ric Murphy. The guy is nuts for you. Unless you want to see if that cutie from Boston College is available.

Gina sighed. Yes, Ric had made it clear since the first night she worked at the bar he was interested in her. And the cutie from Massachusetts was a guy Gina had met on vacation who'd already emailed twice this week.

Both fun guys, both good-looking, both easy to talk to, but neither guy was Justin.

She closed her eyes.

It was time to move on. Pulling up a number before she had time to talk herself out of it, Gina put the phone to her ear. "Hello, Ric? It's Gina. I was wondering if you had any plans for next Saturday night?"

She'd been stood up.

Ric had called an hour ago to tell her he had the flu and wouldn't be able to take her to the dance. All dressed up and nowhere to go.

Gina had kept quiet about her change of plans during the excitement of her mother snapping pictures of the twins and their respective dates in front of the fireplace. Giselle looked lovely standing next to her date in her lemon-yellow chiffon gown with its multilayered tiered skirt. Garrett had returned home after picking up Leenie Harden, his steady girlfriend and the daughter of the mayor, to have their pictures taken. Then the four teenagers left to meet friends and head to the dance.

"Shouldn't your date be here soon?"

Gina looked at her mother. "Ric called a while ago. He's not coming."

"What?"

"He's got the flu. He said it started as a cold and got worse as the day went on. He'd hoped to be able to make it which is why he called so late, but…"

"Oh, honey, I'm sorry. You were so excited about your date."

Gina sighed. "Ric isn't a date. I mean, yes, he was my date tonight, but it's no big deal."

No big deal.

The words echoed inside her head.

Words that had become her mantra in the last two weeks.

Words Justin must've taken to heart because he was back to treating her as a polite acquaintance at best. With his working days and her working nights, it wasn't as if she'd had much of a chance to see him anyway. He wasn't outright ignoring her, but was treating her with cool indifference. As if everything that had happened between them was, indeed, no big deal.

Gina sank to the corner of the couch and closed her eyes, determined not to let her mother see her unexpected tears. Why was she upset? It was just a silly high school dance. So what if she spent a small fortune on the dress and heels?

"You don't have to stick around." Head dipped, Gina slipped off one shoe and wiggled her toes. She'd worn the Betsey Johnson peep toes around the house all week trying to break them in. "I know you and Hank have plans."

"You could still go."

"Show up alone? I don't think so."

"Gina Marie Steele, those children are counting on you." Her mother's tone got the desired results. Gina looked up at her. "Not to mention the other chaperones."

Her mother was right, of course, but she hated the idea of walking into the school gym all by herself. Maybe she could hide out in the girls' restroom. Or roam the halls making sure no one tried to find a dark corner.

"I know, Mom, I know."

"Hank should be here soon. We could take you over to the school on our way to the movies."

Gina offered a half-hearted laugh. "Dropped off at the dance by my mother? No, thanks. I'll drive myself as soon as I change my clothes."

"Change?"

Rising, Gina balanced herself, putting most of her weight on her bare foot. "Yes, change. Getting all dressed up for a date is one thing, but I'm not showing up alone looking like this. I'll put on a simple dress and sensible shoes."

"But, Gina—"

"No buts, Mom. Go powder your pretty nose before your guy gets here."

Gina could see an argument brewing, but her mom turned and disappeared down the hall to her bedroom. Seconds later, the doorbell rang.

"There's Hank. I'll get it," Gina called out before hobbling to the front door. Opening it, she bent and tried to wiggle her bare foot back into the new shoe. "Hey, there. My mom will be just a second…"

Her voice disappeared the moment she noticed the polished cowboy boots shining in the glow of the porch light.

Her eyes flew to his face, but a black Stetson, worn low over his brow, made it impossible to see anything more than his familiar straight nose, full mouth and square jaw.

Justin.

She gave up on her shoe and slowly straightened, clutching the high heel to her chest as she took in his dark suit jacket, matching trousers and stark white shirt. Instead of a standard tie, a bolo tie with a metallic gray stone surrounded by silver scroll work hung around his neck.

Justin Dillon stood on her front porch looking sinfully delicious all dressed up for a night on the town. And in his hands he held a clear plastic corsage box containing a cluster of yellow roses.

"If you're looking for a Prince Charming to help you with that shoe, Cinderella—" the familiar low timbre of his voice stole over her skin "—you're out of luck."

Damn, she was breathtaking.

Bare shoulders, a hint of cleavage where the front of her strapless dress dipped, especially when she'd bent at the waist to play with her shoe. Smooth, bare legs and tiny feet with bright pink toenails to match her hair. Even in a mess of curls piled on her head, he could see the pink streak of color over her left ear.

The desire to kiss those shiny lips, now formed in a perfect O of surprise, surged through him and he knew one undeniable truth.

This was wrong.

This was one hundred percent wrong.

And not just because of what that couple had said to him that night in the library parking lot.

They'd turned out to be Harold Lyons and his wife. Their son had been part of Justin's old crowd years ago until he died of a drug overdose. And as much as he tried to forget their words, a part of him knew they'd spoken the truth. He was flying blind when it came to taking care of a little boy and he certainly didn't have the best role model in his old man in what it took to raise a child.

As for the beautiful lady in front of him...

She'd said she wanted them to be friends, but, hell, that wasn't possible.

He wanted more than just friendship from Gina, except she wasn't a one-time, good-time type of gal. And he wasn't good for anything else.

So he'd stayed clear of her until Racy had arrived at his cabin tonight with this crazy idea. Spending the next couple of hours with Gina while keeping her at a distance was going to be the hardest thing he'd ever done in his life.

"What are you doing here?"

Gina had managed to get her shoe on without his noticing. What he did notice was the surprise in her eyes had turned to suspicion.

"What does it— I'm here to take you to the dance."

Her blue eyes grew wide. "You're what?"

"Your date bailed on you, right?"

"He's sick— Wait, how did you even know I had plans with Ric tonight?"

"You don't think he mentioned your hot date at all this week?" Justin's grip tightened on the plastic container, the crackling noise forcing him to relax. "I knew. Everyone at the bar knew. Ah, hello, ma'am."

Gina's mother smiled from behind her daughter, but Justin could read the surprise on her face at finding him at her front door. "Hello, Justin. My, don't you look nice?"

He nudged the brim of his Stetson upward to look her in the eye. "Thank you, Mrs. Steele."

"Gina, aren't you going to invite him in?"

He could tell it was the last thing she wanted to do. Hell, it was the last thing he wanted, but she stepped aside and waved him in. He walked into the front hall of the Steele home and was immediately greeted by a wall of framed portraits showcasing the entire family, including Gina's late father. Gent Steele had been the sheriff of Destiny for as long as

Justin could remember and a thorn in the side of the Dillon family for years, or vice versa, until his death in a shoot-out a decade ago.

Yeah, Justin was officially out of his comfort zone.

He followed Gina into the living room, his eyes glued to the nape of her bare neck. She stopped in the middle of the room and turned to look at him, her eyes directed at his Stetson.

He used the moment to drop his gaze and look at anything but her. Their home was simple but cozy with more photos, and quilts and pillows in bright reds, greens and black on sturdy leather furniture. It even smelled good, like a mix of fresh flowers and a home-cooked meal.

He'd finally picked up a used living room set last week, but his cabin was far from a family home despite Jacoby's drawings on the refrigerator.

It was then he noticed Gina's mother watching him. Had he ever met a girl's parents before a date? Not that this was a real date, but even as a teenager it wasn't something he ever remembered doing. Not the kind of girls he and his brother Billy used to hang out with.

It seemed she was waiting for him to say something so he went for what he hoped would work. "Ah, you have a nice home."

"Thank you. So, is someone going to tell me what's going on?" Sandy Steele asked as she pulled on a jacket.

"Justin thinks he's a stand-in to keep me from being date-less tonight."

Yeah, that was it in a nutshell, but damn if the way she put it didn't sting a bit. He doubted Gina's mother was going to let her precious daughter out the door with a loser like him anyway, no matter how nicely he polished up—as his sister had put it—on such a simple explanation.

"Oh, well that's nice of you, Justin." Sandy lifted a casserole dish from the nearby dining room table. "Hank called when I was in the back. He's not feeling well either, so it's a DVD and my chicken soup at his place. Oh, would you like me to take your picture before I go?"

Gina waved off her mother's offer. "Mom, I don't even know if I'm going."

Well, that was plain enough. She'd been willing to go with Ric Murphy. Hell, she'd invited him as her date. Now that he'd shown up, all bets were off.

"You know how I feel about that, so I'll just tell you both how lovely you look and say my good-nights." Sandy gave her daughter a kiss on the cheek, then headed around the oversize table. "I'll be home in plenty of time to make sure the twins meet their curfew, so don't feel you need to rush back here after the dance, sweetheart. Justin, please drive carefully."

"Yes, ma'am."

Gina followed her mother through the kitchen. Hushed whispers came from the back door, but he couldn't make out their words. He'd bet a thousand bucks they were talking about him and none of it was good. He turned away and busied himself with looking at even more photos, mostly of the Steele children growing up. He noticed there weren't that many candid shots of Gina. Just the standard annual school pictures of her in a uniform.

Moments later, the clicking of heels and her familiar scent, a spicy and sweet cinnamon fragrance, told him she'd come back into the room.

"Why are you doing this?"

He turned to her, still amazed at how beautiful she looked. "What do you mean?"

"You show up unannounced—" she paused and bit at her lower lip before she continued "—and just expect me to go with you?"

"I don't expect anything."

He heard confusion in her voice, almost as if she thought

she wasn't worthy of getting dressed up and going to the dance.

Or was it just that she didn't want to go with him?

She was right to feel that way. This night had disaster written all over it, but a promise was a promise.

"Racy showed up at my place about an hour ago," Justin said. "She told me about Ric calling out of his afternoon shift because he was sick. I guess she checked on him later and found he was still in bed. She was concerned about you missing this shindig and convinced me— Look, if you want to go to the dance alone, that's fine by me."

She again bit down on her bottom lip. For some crazy reason he found it incredibly sexy, but it was the wariness in her eyes that told him she was either going to do just that—go alone—or skip this event all together.

Either way, he was out of here.

"Well, I've got a beer and a ball game waiting for me." He started past her. "So if you'll excuse me—"

"Wait." She touched his arm, stopping him. "Are those flowers for me?"

Chapter Ten

No big deal.
I can do this.
We're just friends.

Gina's collection of mantras was growing by the minute. Not that any of them helped as she and Justin walked up to the festively decorated entrance to the high school.

Kiss him senseless.

Now there was a mantra she could get behind.

No, she chided herself, there was no kissing between friends. Friends or not, she still couldn't believe Justin had shown up at her house, looking like a *GQ* model for cowboys, to escort her to the dance.

Actually, that wasn't what he'd done. He'd shown up because he promised his sister he would. But did he have to bring her a corsage? Or was that Racy's idea, too?

The yellow rosebuds tickled her wrist, but it was the heat of Justin's hand suddenly against her lower back that caused her to jump.

"You okay?" His hand dropped away.

Gina jerked her head in a quick nod, trying to ignore the quivering in her tummy.

She'd surprised him when she'd agreed to come. Heck, she'd surprised herself, but she couldn't let the fantasy of this evening invade the reality of the situation.

She hadn't wanted to come alone.

Justin hadn't wanted to come at all.

In fact, on the ride here, in the restored 1946 Ford pickup Justin said her brother had insisted they use, Gina had come up with a plan. Check in with the head chaperone, apologize for being thirty minutes late and see if her services were still needed. If not, she'd find the twins, say hello and get out of there.

When they arrived at the double glass doors, their hands collided as they reached for the handle at the same time. She snatched hers back as if burned. Okay, not burned, but his touch certainly made her skin sizzle.

"I think opening the door is my job," Justin said.

She looked at him. He'd left his Stetson in the truck, making it easier to see his face. Not that she could read anything in his stare.

He raised a brow. "What?"

"If you don't want to go inside, I'll understand," she said in a low whisper. "We can say you gave me a ride and leave it at that. I'm sure I can find someone to give me a ride home."

He took a step closer, then dipped his head. His gaze dropped to her mouth for a split second, almost as if he—

She blinked hard and he raised his chin.

"I'm not going anywhere." He pulled open the door and stepped back. "After you, Miss Steele."

Gina walked into the school's brightly lit lobby, the faint sounds of a classic Elvis tune filling the air. A table stood off to one side. Two women around her mother's age sat behind it. One stood when they approached.

"May we help you?" the lady asked.

"Yes, I'm one of the chaperones for tonight's dance. My apologies for arriving late."

The woman, reading glasses perched on the end of her nose, dipped her head. Looking at Gina over the thin black rims, her lips pressed tightly together. "Your name?"

Gina tried not to take the woman's disapproval personally. She lifted her chin and offered a smile. "Gina Steele."

The other woman rose and the two of them looked from her to Justin. The turn of their heads, slight frowns on their faces, and the arching of their eyebrows occurred in perfect unison.

Their silent judgment hung in the air like a dark cloud. Gina recognized the second woman as a member of the town's betterment committee and a close friend of the group's leader, a woman who tried to use the committee to cause trouble for Racy just a few months ago.

"If you could tell me where we can find the senior class sponsor," Gina said, hoping Justin didn't recognize the woman who'd tried to hurt his sister. "We'd appreciate it."

"Mrs. Powers should be in the gymnasium." The same woman spoke while the other reached for a pen and made a notation on a nearby sheet of paper. "It's straight down this hallway, past the cafeteria."

"Do you need to add the name of my escort to your list?"

The second woman jerked up her head. "Ah, yes, of course."

"Dillon. Justin Dillon," he spoke before she could open her mouth, "but you already know who I am, Mrs. Lyons."

Gina looked at him, but he'd turned away. She hurried to join him and they walked down the hall, side by side, but not touching. Gina peeked at him, but Justin stared straight ahead, his jaw clamped tight.

"Boy, schools sure look different at night, don't they?"

Her voice came out a hushed whisper. "Is this the first time you've been back here since you graduated?"

"I never graduated from here. I dropped out the start of my junior year."

Before she could think of a response, they turned a corner, the music louder now, and soon they arrived at the gym. Young people in varying degrees of formal wear, most of the girls dressed like her sister and herself in vintage dresses, stood in small groups in the wide hallway. Curious glances from the teenagers greeted them, but it was the outright stares from the adults that caused Gina to freeze.

Two older gentlemen, one of whom was the football coach, stood at the other end of the hall, directing a line of teenage couples waiting to get their pictures taken. The men were soon joined by two women, probably teachers, as well, and all four spoke in hushed voices. From their furtive glances it was obvious Gina and Justin were the topic of a heated discussion.

"Let's go inside, okay?" Gina clutched her handbag.

Justin waved her ahead of him. It was warm inside the gym, with a faint whiff of sweaty socks in the air. A mirrored ball hung from the ceiling, sprinkling dots of light over crepe-paper swirls in the school colors of blue and white. A stage at the far end held a pair of disc jockeys and an empty set of thrones waiting for the crowning of the king and queen. Teenagers filled the center of the gym as well as the round tables set up alongside the stacked bleachers.

Gina's age discrepancy from her classmates and her own shyness had kept her from ever attending a dance while at her private high school. She'd tried to go to the freshman mixer her first year at college but had only made it as far as the front steps before chickening out and heading back to her dorm room.

She could now see the magic she missed out on, but recapturing a stolen moment wasn't going to happen tonight.

"I think your sister is headed this way." Thanks to the loud music, Justin had to speak right into her ear. The warmth of his breath caused those proverbial tummy quivers to spread to her entire body.

"It's about time you got here." Giselle joined them, dragging along her date by the hand. "Where's your— Ah, hi."

"Ric's home sick with the flu," Gina explained, placing a hand on Justin's arm. His muscles tensed beneath the smooth fabric of his suit and she tightened her grip. To reassure him or herself?

"Justin graciously agreed to stand in as my date tonight." She was babbling, but as always, once she started it was impossible to stop. "He even managed to get Gage to lend us his beloved pickup."

"Wow, that's so cool! Both Garrett and I tried to wrangle the keys to that baby, but he refused." Giselle smiled. "Hey, Justin."

"Hey."

His one word reply had Gina scrambling to put her earlier plan into action. "Giselle, do you know where I can find Mrs. Powers? I think I should check in with her."

"Probably the closest bathroom because she's ready to pop any moment." The tall, muscular, blond teenager standing with Giselle spoke and tugged at his tie at the same time.

"Mrs. Powers is pregnant," Giselle explained, "and her due date is just a week away. Come on, we'll find her."

Gina looked at Justin. "Will you be okay if I—"

"Sure, he will. Justin, this is Stefan Marcuso, my boyfriend." Giselle made a quick introduction. "Stef, Justin Dillon."

The kid stuck out his hand and a heartbeat passed before Justin shook it. Gina let her sister drag her away, hoping he didn't mind being left with the boy.

"So, is it true you did time in prison for dealing?"

Gina cringed at the teenager's question, but the sooner she

checked in the sooner she'd be able to tell Justin his escorting duties were over. Moments later, they found Mrs. Powers outside the girls' restroom. Giselle made introductions and headed back to the gym.

"I'm so sorry I'm late," Gina apologized again. "But I'm here and ready to go to work. What do you need me to do?"

"Actually, our chaperone ranks are pretty full." Linda Powers, a math teacher who served as the senior class adviser, pressed one hand to her extended belly. "So many long-time staff members wanted to participate in the festivity."

Gina studied the mother-to-be and found herself wondering if she, too, held the same contemptuous attitude toward Justin that so many other adults at the dance seemed to. "Oh, well, if you're sure you don't need me—"

"You're welcome to stay—you and your date—and enjoy the dance if you'd like. Excuse me, I need to check on the voting for tonight's royal court."

"Yes, of course."

Gina watched the woman slowly make her way down the hall. She wanted to believe the sincerity of the invitation, but after all they'd experienced from the other adults, she wasn't sure. Needing a moment to collect her thoughts, she slipped inside the ladies' room. In the last stall, she locked the door and leaned against the wall.

Free to go. Free to stay.

She took a few deep breaths, and pushed away the image that popped into her head of her and Justin sharing a slow dance to a classic doo-wop ballad.

Leaving was the best answer for everyone.

She exited the stall and looked at her reflection in the mirror. A quick swipe with the lip gloss and she was ready.

"...but to bring that man here? To a high school dance?" The door opened and the two women Gina had seen earlier with the football coach entered.

"One would think as the sister of our sheriff," the second woman spoke, "not to mention from one of the town's finest families, she'd know better."

"Better than what?" Gina turned and faced them, enjoying the look of shock on their faces.

"Ah, Miss Steele."

"Yes, that's who I am, but I'm afraid I don't know you ladies."

She was surprised her voice sounded so calm. Inside, she was shaking with fury. "Third time's the charm," wasn't that the familiar saying? At the front door, then when they arrived at the gym and now here.

Enough was enough.

"I believe you have an issue with my date?"

The first woman folded her hands in front of her. "Yes, frankly, we do. I'm Beverly Simpson, an English teacher here at the high school. I am also a parent with two children attending this dance and I feel this is the last place a former drug dealer should be."

"Justin has paid his debt for his past behavior. He is working hard to rebuild his life, for both himself and his son."

"And how can we be sure he hasn't reverted to his old ways? Like father, like son, as the saying goes."

"Does that mean we can assume your parents instilled this narrow-mindedness in you?" Gina advanced on the second woman who'd spoken. "Maybe it's best not to stand in judgment on others, lest you be judged yourselves."

"Are you really that sure of him?"

"Yes, I am."

Memories of that night in the bar three months ago came rushing back to Gina. It hadn't taken long for her to realize the men who barged in were old friends of Justin. He'd wanted nothing to do with them or their plans and ended up being hurt while defending her.

She offered the ladies a gentle smile. "Perhaps it's time for a leap of faith, in ourselves and in others."

Gina headed back for the gym. She stopped at one of the refreshment tables and took two cold drinks. With a new-found confidence, she made her way back to where she'd left her date.

He wasn't there.

Ignoring the way her heart skipped a beat, she continued to walk the perimeter of the dance floor. Justin wouldn't just leave, not without saying goodbye. When she finally spotted him, her footsteps faltered. He was sitting at a table in the far corner, surrounded by a group of teenagers, including the twins and their dates.

"Hey, sis." Garrett rose from where he sat next to Justin when she reached the table.

Justin's head swung toward her. He stood. His suit jacket hung from the back of his chair and he'd rolled his shirt sleeves back to below his elbows. Taking the sodas from her, he placed them on the table.

"So what's going on?" she asked, after returning her brother's hug.

"Ah, nothing." Justin shoved his hands into his pockets. "Just talking."

"So you were really that good at running?"

Justin's gaze shifted between her and a kid who spoke from the other side of table twice before he replied. "Ah, yeah, I guess. I was on the varsity track team, running cross country, my sophomore year," he shrugged. "Who knows where it might've led if I hadn't been stupid and dropped out."

"You still run now?" one of the girls asked.

"I've started to get back into it, when I can." Justin paused, then continued when the teenagers remained silent. "I was able to use an outdoor track while in prison, but running in circles surrounded by an electrified fence and guards just wasn't the same."

"But you finished high school and got your college degree while you were in prison," Giselle said. "That's impressive."

He did what?

Surprised, Gina looked at him. He'd told her only an hour ago that he'd never graduated from high school.

From *this* high school.

"It would've been more impressive if I accomplished those things without getting drawn into a world of fast money," Justin replied.

One kid nodded, his face a study in concentration. "My cousin was all set with a big-time basketball scholarship and he blew it, getting too full of his own glory. He thought he could get away with anything. Instead he got busted and lost it all."

"Which is why I steer clear of that crap," said another one of the boys. "Figuring out the future is hard enough, you know?"

"Something none of you have to do tonight." Justin gestured toward the dance floor. "Have a good time, that's what the dance is for. Leave the figuring for tomorrow."

Everyone moved away, most to the dance floor until it was just Gina and Justin at the table.

"You never told me you had a college degree."

Justin slumped back into the closest folding chair. "You never asked."

"Okay." Gina sat next to him. "I'm asking now."

He didn't say anything, so she waited.

"I've got a bachelor's degree in English," he finally responded to her unspoken question. "With minors in Liberal Arts and Humanities."

Her mind flashed back to the overflowing bookcases in the cabin. "That *is* impressive. So, what was all this about? With the kids?"

"Your sister's boyfriend asked me what I did to get sent to prison."

"I know, I heard him."

"It was a nice change to be asked directly instead of all the stares and whispering, so I told him." Justin wrapped a hand around one of the sodas. "Next thing I knew I was surrounded, talking about the stupid things I did as a teenager that led to the stupid things I did as an adult, and the price I paid."

Gina leaned forward and placed her hand on his. "Most people just tell kids what to do or what not to do. I think it probably helped them to actually speak with someone who could share the consequences of his actions."

"Yeah, that's me," Justin scowled, "a 'consequences of my actions' kind of guy."

"You're so much more than that," she protested. "And you know it."

"Do I?" Justin pulled from her touch and popped open the can. He took a long draw before he spoke again. "Just because I share a couple of stories and try to scare these kids into keeping on the straight and narrow doesn't make me a good person."

"You are a good person. You came tonight even though this is the last place you wanted to be. You've put up with the rudeness of so many people so I wouldn't have to face walking into this event by myself." She paused and swallowed hard before she continued. This was the last thing she wanted to say, but it was only fair. "So, if you want to go, it's okay."

He turned to look at her. "What?"

"We're free to leave." Now she was the one to look away, her focus on a small candle flickering in the center of the white linen tablecloth. "I guess they've got enough chaperones to keep the kids in line, we're not needed."

"Or wanted."

She shrugged and tried not to show how much what was

probably a correct assumption bothered her. "It's no big deal."

Biting on her bottom lip couldn't stop the words from slipping out, but at least it muffled most of her groan. Of all the words in the English language, why did she pick those four?

She was wrong. It was a big deal.

Ever since they'd left her house tonight, Gina had been working overtime to maintain an invisible barrier between them because she had to have known the kind of reactions they'd get showing up together. And those reactions were bothering her more than she was willing to admit.

Not that Justin blamed her. She didn't deserve them. Or his chilly attitude since the moment she'd surprised him by agreeing to come here tonight with him.

What had he told those kids? To enjoy themselves? And here he was, so wrapped up in his own issues that he'd failed to make sure Gina enjoyed this night, too. He stared at her, waiting until she looked at him again. She finally bowed to the silent pressure and glanced up through her lashes.

"You're amazing, you know that?"

Her beautiful blue eyes widened as she turned fully toward him with those damn shiny lips open in surprise.

"You're the one who's had to put up with the disrespect of these people tonight…because of me." He stopped her un-voiced protest with a wave of his hand and scooted his chair closer until he bracketed her legs with his. "If you'd shown up with Ric, everyone would be smiling and happy, *you'd* be smiling and happy. Instead, you got stuck with someone who can't even hold a pleasant conversation, much less— Look, staying or leaving isn't my call, it's yours."

Justin cut off his tirade and pulled in a deep breath. "From this moment on, this night is about what you want. So what's it going to be?"

She opened her mouth, but quickly closed it again. He leaned in, knowing he shouldn't touch her, but still he ran the tip of his finger along her jaw. "Don't think. Just go with the first thing that comes to your mind. What do you want?"

"I want to dance."

Of all the possible answers, that was the last thing he'd expected her to say.

He straightened. "You want to what?"

"I want to dance," she repeated softly, "with you."

He grabbed her hand and pulled her to her feet as a rock and roll classic pounded through the speakers.

"Justin, are you sure you want to do this? Dance with me?"

"More than anything."

That was a lie. What he wanted to do more than anything was kiss her, but her smile, wide and full of life, captured him. It was the first time he'd seen that smile in almost two weeks. In fact, the last time was when she'd held his son's simple crayon drawing in her hands.

His son.

Thanks to a delay from the laboratory he'd found out just this afternoon that Jacoby was indeed his flesh and blood. Justin hadn't been surprised. Deep inside, he'd known the boy was his. The sudden urge to share his news with Gina filled him, but he decided to wait until they could talk without music blaring. He tightened his grip on her hand and led her to the crowded dance floor.

When she turned to face him, he said, "Are you sure about this? Two-stepping is more my speed. I don't think I can swing, or jitterbug, or whatever kind of dancing goes with ol' time rock and roll."

Gina pressed her cheek to his, her lips moving against to his ear. "Like these kids do? This music belongs to their grandparents. Just have fun!"

It was fun, all of it, from the crazy songs to the teenagers bouncing around them, to being able to hold Gina's hands in his as they did their own version of cutting loose. It took him until the second song before he stopped caring if others watched, and as he'd advised the teens, he enjoyed himself. He hadn't relaxed like this in a long time and being able to share it with Gina made it even more special.

When a slow ballad finally came on, Gina slipped into his arms. He wanted to press her close, to feel her curves against his chest. Then he noticed they were being watched by her brother and sister who were close by, dancing with their dates.

"We're not officially chaperones," Gina said. "But we should probably display the proper decorum."

"Have you checked out the couples around us? No one else is dancing with enough room between them for a third party."

"Would you like to sit this one out instead?"

Justin grinned and shook his head. "No, I have a much better idea."

Chapter Eleven

Justin kept Gina's hand in his as he led her off the dance floor. Moving her in front of him, he steered her back to the table, but only long enough to grab his jacket. Gina shot him a look but kept walking. They slowly made their way around the outer rim of the tables until they reached a shadowed cove between the stacked bleachers.

She halted. "Where are we going?"

"Trust me."

He tugged on her hand and made his way to the double doors he'd used years ago to sneak out of school. Only one thing could get in the way— Ah, still no fire alarm attached.

Perfect.

In fact, the doors had been propped open to allow a cool breeze to enter the stuffy gym. He eased outside, pausing to make sure they weren't interrupting someone else with the same idea. Nope, they were alone.

The night air felt good against his heated skin. "Much better."

"Where are we?" Gina shivered slightly in the light breeze. "And why?"

He let go of her long enough to drape his suit jacket over her bare shoulders. "The far side of the gym. This road leads from the front parking lot to the athletic fields around the back."

She tucked her tiny purse into the inside pocket of his jacket, then slipped her arms into the sleeves. Justin grinned as she rolled the long cuffs back to her wrists.

"And the woods are beyond that," she said. "Something tells me you've used this exit before. Reliving a bit of your youth, Mr. Dillon?"

Justin took her hand again and moved back into the shadows. "No, I never snuck out here with a pretty girl."

The music from inside the gym was muted but could still be heard. He dragged her up against his body, putting one hand beneath his jacket to the small of her back, and pressed her close. He brought their joined hands to rest against his chest. Her free hand went to his shoulder, her touch warm through his shirt.

Maybe this wasn't the best idea.

Hell, he was pushing his luck holding her like this, but her conviction that he was a good person had got to him. Got to a place he'd buried so deep, he couldn't even find it anymore. He'd tried to keep a wall between them, but this lady—one part vixen, one part angel—kept finding ways to get past it. He should've walked away when she gave him the chance, but he wanted to stay and give her the night she deserved.

Now selfishly, he was doing something he'd wanted to do for the past hour, hold her in his arms away from the crowds and spying eyes. A moment alone, just the two of them, and if he found the courage, he was going to kiss her.

Despite every fiber of his being telling him it was the last thing in the world he should do, he wanted to kiss Gina. A full-contact, wet-tongued, bone-melting kind of kiss. Like the one they'd shared in the dark of his kitchen. The one he couldn't get out of his head.

"I heard the good news the other day."

Justin stilled. Good news? Was she talking about Jacoby? No, wait—she said *the other day*. "What good news?" he asked.

"About your friend, Bobby Winslow? Racy said it looks like he's going to recover from that horrific car crash."

"Yeah, he's going to be in the hospital for a while, and there's a lot of talk about whether he'll be able to get behind the wheel of a race car again, but he'll survive. That's the most important thing."

Gina dipped her head to rest it on his shoulder. "Gage said all Bobby ever wanted to do was be a race car driver. It must be so hard knowing he might have to give up his dream."

Justin wouldn't know about that. He'd given up on his own dreams long ago. Then again, holding this lady in his arms felt about as close to a dream as one could get.

"Is this okay? Dancing out here?" The softness of her hair brushed against his chin and tickled his nose. He pulled in a deep breath and her signature scent wrapped around him as they moved. "We can go back inside if you want."

"What I want," Gina whispered, her breath warm against his neck, "is to be right here, like this, with you."

An emotion he couldn't describe filled his chest. Pride? Pleasure? He didn't know and he didn't care. He didn't want to think, just feel and let the rest of the world disappear.

Except for one small thing he wanted to share with her right this very minute. "Guess what? I finally got the DNA test results back. Jacoby is my son."

Gina's smile was serene. "Of course he is. Congratulations, anyway."

"You didn't have any doubt?"

"Not once."

Not sure how to reply to her confident tone, he stayed quiet as they moved in a silent embrace as one song ended and another began.

Gina's fingers gently traveled to the large stone at the center of his bolo tie. "I remember this. You wore it at Racy and Gage's renewal ceremony."

"Same suit and boots, too." His words came out in a rough whisper. He had to pause and clear his throat. "The tie once belonged to my grandfather. Racy found it in an old box years ago, long after my father died and Billy Joe and I— Well…"

Surprised at how much he wanted to share this story with her, he continued, "Racy gave it to me the day she and Gage renewed their vows. I told her she should give it to her husband, but she insisted it stay in the family. Someday, I'll pass it down to Jacoby, I guess. Maybe he'll want to wear it to his senior prom."

Gina's fingers traced the braided leather cords that hung from the tie to lie against his shirt. Her touch sent a burning sensation through him. He flexed his fingers at her back to keep from crushing her to his chest.

"Well, you look very handsome wearing it."

He used their linked fingers to lift her chin until he could see her eyes. "I know I haven't said it, and I'm a fool for waiting so long, but you look beautiful tonight."

Thanks to the shadows it was hard to see the now-familiar pink blush on her cheeks, but he was sure it was there. "Yes, it's a pretty dress—"

"It's not the dress. It's you, Gina."

She pulled from his touch and looked away. He untangled their fingers, his hand cupping the nape of her neck. The slightest pressure had her looking at him again.

"It's your smile, your eyes and this bright pink in your hair you keep trying to hide." It took only a tug of his index finger to set the curl free and it fell to rest along her neck and the collar of his jacket. "There, much better."

"Justin..."

His thumb stroked across her lips, stopping her words. He lowered his head until their foreheads touched. "This has got to be the craziest thing I've done in a long time, but right now I want to—"

A muffled cry broke the night air. Both Justin and Gina stilled.

"What was that?" she whispered. "An animal?"

"Shh...wait..."

There it was again. Justin recognized the sound this time. He released Gina, pushing past her. "Go back inside. Now."

"Justin, what is it?"

"Someone's in trouble." He started for the far corner of the building, heading deeper into the dark. Gut instincts, honed to a razor's edge thanks to his time behind bars, kicked in. Whatever was going on, it wasn't good. "Just go."

"And leave you alone? No way."

Gina caught up with him as they rounded the corner. He wanted to yell at her to listen to him, but the scene in front of them caused Justin to grab her and they froze.

Twenty feet away, two seniors and their dates, obviously from the dance from their tuxedos and gowns, were in a world of trouble with four men, clearly intruders from their scruffy jeans, T-shirts and hooded sweatshirts.

Two of the hoodlums held one boy captive despite his struggles to break free, a bandana jammed into his mouth. A pretty blonde girl was held by a third man, his hand pressed tightly over her mouth. The last goon was squared off with another partygoer, a young kid in a white tuxedo, built like a football player, who stood between his visibly scared date and the shiny glint of a switchblade.

Justin turned to Gina and gestured to her to make a phone

call. She reached inside the jacket for her purse, but he couldn't wait. He raced across the grass, shoving the tuxedo-clad kid to the ground as the thug with the knife lunged.

Surprise crossed the knifer's face at his sudden appearance and Justin sucked in his stomach, but the sharp edge sliced twice at his shirt. Adrenaline pulsing through his veins, he swung out his right leg, striking with his foot and sending the knife flying into the night sky. Before the guy could recover, Justin threw a quick fist to the jaw and the guy was flat on his back.

"Justin! Look out!"

He turned, with barely enough time to plant his feet before being charged by the thug who'd let go of the girl to come after him. He used the man's forward motion against him, but they both went sprawling into the dirt. This one was bigger and managed to place a few punches, but Justin fought back and when the opening came, he knocked the wind out of the jerk with a well placed right hook.

Knowing there were two other goons to deal with, Justin struggled to his feet, only to find they'd released the other teen and took off. Red-and-blue lights flashed, and seconds later a deputy sheriff's cruiser rounded the far corner of the building, blocking their escape. Chaperones and teenagers spilled out of the nearby double doors.

That fast, it was over.

Justin winced as he stood, a little unsteady on his feet when Gina raced to his side. "Ohmigod, are you okay?"

She reached for him, but he only grabbed her hand and held on tight. "I'm…fine," he punched out between gutted breaths. "What about…the kids?"

It took a few moments and most of the adults to get the curious onlookers back inside the gym. Then it was only the coach, another male teacher and Mrs. Powers left, along with the sheriff's deputy, who'd been patrolling the parking lot when the call came in. Volunteer EMTs arrived next and right behind them, the sheriff.

"Gina!" Gage stepped out of his Jeep. "Are you all right? What's going on here?"

Justin lessened his grip, but Gina held on tight and stayed by his side as her brother approached. Gina quickly filled him in on what had happened, ending with her assurance that as far as she knew both Giselle and Garrett were safe inside the gym.

Gage gave Justin a long stare before he walked away to talk with his deputy, who had the four assailants sitting on the ground by a chain-link fence. The EMTs checked out the teenagers and the four attackers who were then handcuffed and squeezed in to the back of the cruiser.

"You kids came out for some fresh air and then this group showed up?" Gage addressed the teens.

The one who'd had the cloth jammed into his mouth nodded, tightening his arm around the weeping girl next to him. "Yes, sir. They just appeared out of the dark. They must've come from the football field."

He went on to explain how they asked for money and when the teens refused and tried to head back inside, things got ugly. His friends backed up his story, repeating what they'd already told the deputy, who with the okay from Gage, headed to the jail with the assailants.

"Michael?"

A woman's high voice had everyone turning toward the doors. Justin recognized her as one of the chaperones who'd given him and Gina a look of disdain earlier tonight.

"Oh, Michael!" She rushed forward and pulled the boy in the dirt-stained white tux into her arms. "Your sister just told me what happened." She released the boy long enough to wrap one arm around the girl next to him. "Oh, sweetie, are you okay?"

"We're fine, Mrs. Simpson," the girl said.

"Yes, they are," Gage agreed, jerking a thumb in Justin's direction, "thanks to that guy."

Ten pairs of eyes locked on him at once, but the ones he was most interested in were a vivid shade of blue. He looked down at Gina and saw concern and admiration in those cerulean depths, along with the sparkle of unshed tears.

"Hey, it's okay," he whispered when she blinked, releasing one of those tears. He quickly brushed it away with the pad of his thumb over her cheekbone. "It's all over."

"But you could've been hurt…" Her voice trailed off as she wrapped her arms around his waist, leaving him no choice but to put his arm across her shoulders.

Ignoring the slice of pain across his midsection, Justin tightened his hold and turned to look at her brother. His face also held concern and admiration. Justin knew the sheriff's concern was for Gina and the way she held on to him, but the respect aimed his way? That was a surprise.

"Thank you, sir." Michael walked to Justin and held out his hand. "I don't know what would've happened if you didn't show up." He shrugged, then continued, "I figured it was going to be a plain ol' fist fight. That I could've handled, but I was out of my element when I saw that knife."

"Hey, you got between danger and your girl. You put her safety and well-being ahead of yours," Justin said, taking his hand. "That was a very brave thing to do."

The kid straightened his shoulders and Justin could see his words had the desired effect on the teen's fragile ego.

The kid nodded and seconds later, Justin found himself accepting the appreciation of all the adults with a handshake and a quick nod. It was surreal, considering the way these people had treated him and Gina earlier in the evening. In his younger days, he probably would've told them to take their thank-yous and shove them where the sun don't shine.

Now, he accepted them, making sure to point out it was Gina's phone call that got the law there quickly. Then everyone headed back inside until it was only Justin, Gina and Gage standing outside.

"You two going back to finish chaperoning?" Gage asked.

Good question. Justin had no idea what they were going to do, but he sure could use a couple of aspirin and a stiff drink. "Ah, I don't know—"

"We're just going to enjoy the rest of our evening," Gina interrupted Justin, "by ourselves."

"I've got to head to the station and call Racy to let her know you're both okay."

"How's Jacoby?" Justin asked.

"Curled up on the sofa watching a movie and fighting sleep when I left. We plan to take him to church with us in the morning, if that's okay with you?"

Justin nodded.

Gage started for his Jeep, but stopped to lightly slap his brother-in-law on the back. "You did a good thing here tonight, Dillon. There just might be hope for you yet."

Gina watched Justin slowly climb behind the wheel. He'd taken back his jacket at her insistence even though he'd told her the slight trembles he was experiencing were a delayed reaction to the fight. He was lying. He was hurt. She could feel it in the way he'd gripped her shoulder earlier and the sharp intake of breath when she'd squeezed him.

"So, where to next?" He buckled the old-fashioned seat belt across his lap and started the engine. Pulling from the parking lot, he headed toward Main Street. "Want to get something to eat? We could go by the diner. I'm guessing they'll be overrun with teenyboppers in another couple of hours."

"How about your place?"

Justin hit the brakes for the red light at the intersection a bit too hard. When the truck stopped, he swung his head to look at her. Despite his best effort, she noticed from the corner of her eye that the movements made him flinch.

"My place?"

Proud at how casual her words came out, Gina smoothed out the skirt of her dress. "Of course, we could go back to my house, but my mother might be home by now."

"Ah, n-no," Justin croaked, then cleared his throat. "My place is fine."

She angled to face him, as much as her own seat belt would allow, and lifted his Stetson from where it lay between them to rest it on her lap. Leaning forward, she slowly walked two fingers up the length of his arm from his wrist to shoulder.

"You know, there's something at your place that both of us really need," she said.

He looked at her through hooded eyes. "What's that?"

She bit back the first response that popped into her head, despite the longing that hummed in her veins. With pouted lips, she returned his stare, lashes fluttering. "A first-aid kit."

He groaned and closed his eyes.

A quick horn toot from the car behind him made Justin put his attention back on the road. He continued to drive, and Gina faced forward again, stunned she'd actually pulled that off.

"How did you know?" he finally asked.

"I'm smart, remember?"

"Gina, it's no big deal." He sighed. "You don't have to do this, I'll be fine."

"It's your place or the clinic." She gestured at the turnoff to the lake. "Or do I make another 9-1-1 call?"

He glared at her, but she only returned his look and re-leased the catch on the sequined flap of her purse. Justin put on the left directional signal and headed for the cabin. Moments later, they were inside and Justin stripped off his jacket. Letting it fall to the floor, he headed for the kitchen and flipped on the overhead lights.

Gina picked up the jacket and headed for the bathroom. Hanging it on a hook on the back of the door, she found a first-aid kit beneath the sink. She then grabbed two towels, wetting the smaller one with warm soapy water.

Walking back into the main room, she halted, noticing the new furniture for the first time. A sofa and loveseat faced the fireplace and a larger television sat atop a nearby cabinet. Simple end tables held mismatched lamps and a coffee table was covered with magazines, a drawing tablet and a tin full of crayons. A round dining room table and four chairs sat nearby in front of the row of windows. All of it was clearly secondhand purchases and while the place still needed something Gina couldn't quite put her finger on, it was easy to see Justin was working hard to make a home for himself and his son.

"What do you think?" He returned from the kitchen, his bolo tie gone and the top buttons of his shirt undone, a bottle of whiskey and two glasses in his hands. "None of it's new, but—"

"I think it's great." She joined him at the couch and made room on the coffee table for the items she'd brought from the bathroom. "I also think we're going to need a bit more light."

He clicked on one lamp, the sudden brightness causing her to blink, but for the first time she could see the slash marks and spots of blood on his shirt.

"Oh, Justin."

He backed away from her outstretched hand and set the glasses next to the first-aid kit. Quickly pouring a splash of whiskey in each, he straightened and offered her one. "Thirsty?"

Gina shook her head. He couldn't look at her. His eyes moved to the glass in his hand before darting around the cabin. Then it hit her. Having her in his home again was driving him crazy. But was it a good crazy or a bad crazy?

She now realized he'd been fighting an attraction to her as much as she'd been fighting what she felt for him. But she'd heard the longing in his voice, felt the restrained desire when he held her while they danced, in the gentleness of his touch when he wiped away her tears.

He didn't want this—whatever *this* was between them— and he was fighting it with everything he had. The question now was what was she going to do about it? What would happen if she and Justin gave in to the powerful magnetic pull they seemed to have toward each other?

Would it be magical or the biggest mistake of their lives?

And was she willing to take the risk of falling even deeper for a guy, who according to all common sense was one hundred percent wrong for her?

"You sure?" he asked again, tipping the whiskey-filled glass toward her, finally looking at her.

This time she nodded. Yes, she was sure.

"Suit yourself." He lifted the glass in a mock toast, then tossed back a mouthful.

Gina took the opportunity to move in closer and quickly unbuttoned his shirt. Two quick yanks and the material was free from his pants and hung open.

"Hey!" He tried to swallow and choked.

"Like I haven't seen this before? Please." Gina tried to play it cool as she pushed his shirt open, but the twin red marks that covered his well-defined stomach from midchest to his waist made her cringe. "Oh, my…you know, this would work better if you lay down."

She looked up at him in time to see Justin toss back the rest of his drink.

"Fine, have it your way."

She dropped to the couch, crinolines and tulle puffing

out around her. His belly button and the faint hairline that disappeared beneath his belt buckle were right in front of her. She grabbed the soapy towel and pressed it to his skin.

"Geez…" Justin released the word in a long hiss.

"You're not even bleeding. Don't tell me this stings." When he didn't reply she looked up and found her gaze locked with his. "Well? Does it?"

A heartbeat passed before he spoke. "No."

Breaking free of his hypnotic hold, she focused again on the toned stomach muscles that twitched beneath her fingers. She moved the cloth with gentle pressure. "Is it cold?"

"No."

"Then what are you complaining about?"

Justin dropped the empty glass to the couch cushion beside her, and pulled her to her feet, the towel falling from her hand. "Tell me you aren't as innocent as you sound. Do you have any idea what you're doing to me?"

"I don't—"

He released her, his hands moving low over her waist until they reached her backside. He pressed her intimately against the junction of his thighs. "This, this is what you do to me."

Biting her bottom lip to hold back a triumphant smile, Gina grabbed on to his dress shirt. His eyes were glued to her mouth, making it impossible for her not to soothe the self-inflicted bite mark with a swipe of her tongue.

Did he just growl?

"Then maybe you should finish what you started at the dance," she whispered. Feeling a new boldness, Gina pushed up on her tiptoes, her hips shifting in a natural rhythm against him as her mouth stopped inches from his.

"Meaning what?"

"You were going to kiss me before we were interrupted."

"Kissing you in public, fully clothed, is a lot different than kissing you here." Justin dropped his head, his lips warm on her bare shoulder. "Or here." He trailed his mouth to the curve of her neck, gently nipping. "Or here."

Gina tried and failed to hold back a low mewl when his lips reached her ear, the heat of his tongue circling the outer shell. "We're—we're still clothed now."

"Not for long."

His warning, spoken against her lips before he took her mouth, caused her heart to pound wildly. He tasted dark and dangerous, like the smooth whiskey on his tongue and the cool night air that clung to his skin. She wound her arms around his neck, fingers curling into the thick strands of his hair. He angled his head to deepen the kiss, more demanding and greedy now. She welcomed him with the quick swipes of her tongue against his.

This kiss was more passionate, more carnal and more decadent than the one they'd shared a few weeks ago, if that was even possible. It burned hotter and brighter, causing a rush of desire to sizzle through every inch of her. His mouth left hers and she gasped for air, instantly missing his touch. Then his lips moved to her other shoulder, his tongue leaving a moist trail to her collarbone. Her eyes drifted closed as she cradled his head in her hands and arched her back as he moved lower.

Was she directing him? She didn't know or care. All she knew was she didn't want him to stop.

Chapter Twelve

Justin moaned when he reached the end of warm, soft skin and the scratchy material of Gina's dress scraped against his chin. It also rasped over his chest and stomach, roughing the already tender skin, but he didn't care. Gina was in his arms, warm, willing and wanton.

He was in heaven.

The swell of her breasts rose from the front of her dress, even more so when she leaned back in his arms. He moved his lips over her skin, pausing to breathe in her spicy scent. The skirt's ruffled layers kept him from fully appreciating the curves he held on to, so he crept one hand up her back, searching for the zipper.

Nothing. Disappointment coursed through him. Realizing his self-control was hanging on by a rapidly unraveling thread, he straightened, lifted his head and bracketed his hands on Gina's waist to set her away from him. When she met his gaze, he read an intense longing in her eyes and fought hard against giving in to the need to kiss her again.

"Gina…"

Her hands drifted from his jaw to rest against his chest, her bright pink fingernails scraping against his skin.

"Gina, you need to be sure—"

She leaned forward and pressed her lips to his chest. "Have I done something to give you the impression I'm not?"

No, she hadn't, but he wanted—no, *needed*—to be certain she knew exactly where this was headed.

Justin bit back a groan when the wet heat of her tongue danced over his nipples. Damn, he hadn't planned this. Not that the thought of making love to her hadn't crossed his mind when he'd showered and gotten dressed tonight.

Hell, the idea of having this lady in his arms, in his bed, had been permanently etched in his brain ever since that night she'd crawled beneath his sheets at his old apartment almost four months ago.

"If you're in too much pain—oh, look at you," Gina gasped and stepped back, her light touch skimming down his chest.

His stomach muscles jumped beneath her fingers. He looked down at the minor red scrapings that melded with the faint cuts from the knife.

"My dress did that to you! I am so sorry. I didn't even think I might be hurting you."

"You're hurting me, all right," he ground out when her fingertips curled into the waistband of his dress pants causing a spike of heat to hit low in his gut. "But it's a beautiful pain, darlin'."

That pretty pink blush he'd come to love stained her cheeks. She looked at him, brushing her thumb across his bottom lip. "I want to stay…with you. If you want me."

"Want is not the question," Justin said, before he captured her finger between his lips and gently sucked. "Even with all those layers, I think you can tell how much I want you."

Her other thumb stayed hooked into his waistband, but her

fingers caressed the hard ridge pressing against his zipper. "Oh, you mean this?"

The teasing glint in her eyes fueled the fire deep inside him. It would be so easy to sweep her into his arms and carry her into his bedroom. "Yeah, that."

"So what are we waiting for?"

Justin wished he knew.

He'd never delayed his need for a woman before in his life. But other than that drunken haze right after his release, he hadn't been with anyone for months. There'd been plenty who'd made it clear they were willing, but it didn't matter. Ever since the night he'd held Gina in his arms, trying to show her how to hold a pool cue, he hadn't wanted anyone else.

The feel of her stepping backward snapped Justin out of his thoughts. She leaned over and clicked off the lamp.

"I can't make any promises," he said.

Where the hell had that come from? And why did it seem easier to say it in the semidarkness?

She didn't speak, only reached for his hand and led him to his bedroom. He followed willingly, but stopped when she did just inside the doorway of the moonlit room.

"Oh, isn't this nice."

Gina dropped his hand and moved to the end of the queen-size sleigh bed that filled the space, her hand sliding along the polished footboard. He'd found the frame while cleaning out the cabin and had spent weeks refinishing it to its former glory. Looking at it now, with its curved head and footboard and high side rails, he saw the bed with new eyes.

Gina's skin would glow against the dark green sheets, reminders of the forest outside the glass doors that filled one wall. The cushioned pillows would cradle her head while he lay between her thighs, and would pad his shoulders as she sat astride him, her legs on either side of his hips—

He crossed to her, needing to get his hands on her again. She turned and met him with a searing kiss. Her hands pushed the shirt off his shoulders and it slid to the floor. Seconds later, her hands released the button on his pants.

"Gina—" He murmured against her lips as he grabbed her trembling fingers.

"I'm not asking for promises, Justin." She returned the gentle squeeze he'd given her hands. "Just love me. Here... now, tonight."

That he could do.

He linked one hand with hers and slowly spun her until they were facing a full-length, standing mirror. Then he gently removed the corsage of yellow roses from her wrist.

"Please be careful with those," she whispered, her gaze locked on their reflection. "I plan on keeping them."

Her words stole his ability to speak.

Justin only nodded and placed the flowers on the dresser. He then lowered his mouth to her bare skin, unable to resist the temptation any longer. They hadn't turned on any lights, but the moonlight streaming through the double glass doors allowed him to easily see her watching his every move in the mirror.

He trailed his fingers up her arms as his lips made their way to her neck, past that bright pink curl. He removed the pins holding the rest of those curls in place. Seconds later, her hair was loose and free.

"You know," he whispered, "It's been driving me crazy all night wondering what you're wearing underneath this dress."

"Not much."

His guttural moan vibrated against her curls as she led his hand to the zipper that started just beneath one arm.

Ah, so that's where it was.

His fingers gently pulled the tiny slider down until it stopped just past her hip. Her hands held the dress to her breasts, but the back opened, revealing nothing but smooth skin and a scrap of black lace.

His gaze locked with hers again in the mirror. Expecting to read shyness in her gaze, the steamy desire he saw instead raced like liquid fire through his veins. He reached out and partially yanked a curtain across the doors, still allowing moonlight to fill the room.

"I thought you didn't like curtains."

"Privacy has its good points, too."

He cupped her chin, turning her head until their lips met. Her kisses were like a drug and he couldn't get enough of them.

She relaxed against him, and he slowly inched the dress from her body. Breaking free to allow her to step out of the garment, he paused to savor the sight of her. His gaze traveled down the natural curve of her back to her tapered waist, lingered on her backside dressed with sheer black lace before moving on to her amazing legs.

"I'll put your dress over here." He started to turn away. "I don't want anything…to happen…to…it…."

Gina did a slow turn to face him, her stomach quivering wildly as Justin lost his ability to speak. He handled her dress with care as he laid it over a nearby chair, his eyes never leaving her as she stood naked except for lace panties, high heels and moonlight.

Her first instinct was to cover herself, but she fought it off. Leaning against the footboard, hands clenched tightly to the curved wood behind her, she instinctively sucked in her tummy, her breasts tingling from the hard breath he exhaled.

"No f-fair." Her words came out in a husky whisper, but it was the best she could do when she saw the need in his eyes. "You have more clothes on than me."

His mouth rose in a half grin and her heart raced. Oh, she loved that smile. He so rarely displayed it, except lately, and she guessed she could thank the new direction his life had taken for that.

"I can fix that."

His eyes caressed her, from her wild curls to the tips of her toes, as he quickly slipped off one cowboy boot, then the other, followed by his socks. Straightening, his eyes locked with hers. He lowered the zipper of his pants and pushed them past his hips. They fell to the floor and he kicked them away.

Giving in to the temptation, she looked at him, all of him, standing before her in snug black boxer briefs that outlined the evidence of his arousal.

"Fair enough?" he asked.

No, it wasn't fair.

It wasn't fair that he was so well put together from the defined muscles of his broad shoulders and strong arms to his long tapered legs. It wasn't fair his beautiful body was marred by the two faint marks across his washboard abs and chiseled hip bones, and it most definitely wasn't fair that she was most likely only going to have this one night with him.

Gina stifled the anguish that insight caused, determined to follow the decision she'd made the moment he'd kissed her. Enjoy tonight. Take this moment, with this man, and live every minute of it.

She returned his smile and pointed the toe of one high heel at him. "Hmm, I think I have the advantage now."

"Not for long." Justin repeated the same line he'd said in the living room as he lifted her into his arms.

The move surprised Gina, but Justin swallowed her squeal with a hard kiss. The bedsheets were cool against her skin as he laid her down and stretched out next to her, never taking his mouth from hers.

After what seemed forever, he pulled away to move to the end of the bed. He lifted each foot and slowly removed her shoes. She wiggled her toes in appreciation, but they curled of their own volition when he placed a kiss at one ankle while his hand curved behind her calf.

His lips never left her skin as they moved up the length of her leg, his fingers repeating the path on the other until he reached the patch of lace covering the most intimate part of her. His breath was hot as he nuzzled her and she was sure he could feel the dampness clinging to her. She reached for his shoulder, whether to pull him farther up her body or to keep him in place she didn't know, while her other hand fluttered over her stomach.

He captured her fingers as his tongue left a moist path between her belly button and the top edge of her panties. "Well, well…what do we have here?"

Gina's breath caught, unsure of how he would react to the words inked above her left hip bone. While enjoying Miami's South Beach on the way back from her vacation, she'd walked into a local tattoo shop, shocking everyone, including herself.

He read the words aloud. "'I shall not live in vain.'"

"It's from an Emily Dickinson poem. I love her work, but this one is my favorite." The words tumbled from her lips. "'If I can stop one heart from breaking, I shall not live—'"

"I know how it goes."

He made his way up her body reciting aloud the poem she'd found years ago while searching for solace in the aftermath of her father's death. Each word was punctured with a kiss, across her stomach, rib cage and the far side of one breast until he stretched out on top of her and whispered the final word against her lips.

She loved him.

As simply and easily as that, Gina fell into the unknown and scary world of truly loving a man. One hundred percent, wholly and completely, head over heels and topsy-turvy in love.

With Justin Dillon.

She closed her eyes against the revelation, afraid he'd be able to see the emotion in her eyes. Pressing into his pillows, she inhaled, and his clean, earthy male scent filled her head.

A low moan escaped as first his hands and then his lips caressed her breasts until he took one nipple into the warm, wet heat of his mouth. She gasped at the sensation, her nails digging into his shoulders. His fingers moved over her skin, lower and lower until they slipped beneath the edge of her panties to stroke her. She mirrored his action, reaching inside his briefs to cup his hard, silky flesh. One stroke, then two, before he pulled from her touch. Seconds later he dispensed of their underwear and they were skin to skin.

Justin was going crazy.

Gina's natural and instinctual moves were driving him insane with desire. He wanted to touch her, kiss her everywhere. She clung to him and he longed to bring her a higher pleasure than she'd ever known before.

"Justin, please."

Her soft cry pierced his heart. He captured her mouth again while reaching for the drawer in the bedside table. He fumbled for one of the packets he'd purchased weeks ago, never really believing he'd have this woman in his arms, in his bed. He quickly sheathed himself and moved between her open legs.

Lowering himself slowly, he wanted to give her time to accept all of him. "I don't…I don't want to hurt—"

"You won't…please."

She tilted her hips, allowing him to ease into her. Her hands moved low on his back, one long smooth leg wrapping around him and their bodies joined.

Powerful emotions crashed over him. A longing to stay, a desire to belong, of being wanted and needed for all the right reasons. He looked at her then and their eyes held. He slid even deeper inside and she rose to meet him. Again and again they moved in perfect unison until she shuddered and cried out his name. And still he couldn't get enough of her. He never wanted the sensations to end, but his body demanded release and he soon found it in the warmth and protection of her body.

Justin's hands shook.

He clenched the small paring knife in one, the fresh pineapple in the other. He'd been up since dawn, working for the last hour on the delicate yet edible flowers. Pineapple daisies, tomato roses, strawberry fans and apple leaves.

He wanted everything to be perfect.

The vanilla crepes were done, filled with fresh blueberries and topped with whipped cream. Freshly squeezed orange juice and coffee were on the breakfast tray, as well. All he needed was to get these last few flowers done and he could get back to his bedroom, to his bed, before Gina woke up.

A deep breath and he went back to work. Stifling a yawn from his sleepless night, he was exhausted but in a good way. He and Gina had turned to each other during the night, making love twice more before she fell into a deep sleep in his arms. He'd closed his eyes, loving the feel of her, wanting to stay there forever.

That's when he'd left the bed.

Being with Gina had been good—no, great, amazing, mind blowing—and he had no idea what to do about it.

They'd agreed last night in the dark to no promises, but in the light of day he had no idea what that meant.

Or where they should go from here.

No, that wasn't true. He did know where they were going.

Nowhere.

Even as he lost a little bit of himself with every kiss, every touch, he knew the fantasy of last night had to come to an end. But he wanted to give her something special, a few more hours of togetherness before the real world barged back into their lives.

A world filled with uncertainties and doubts, fueled by his own battered childhood and his lack of skills needed to raise a child. A world where their pasts dictated their futures, whether they liked it or not.

The ex-con and the egghead? Not likely.

Mentally scraping all of that to one side, he arranged the fruit flowers on the plates. After washing his hands, he grabbed the tray and headed back to the bedroom. He paused at the doorway, enjoying the view of Gina's curls fanned out over his pillows and her curves pressed against the sheets.

Ignoring the way his heart seemed to flip over in his chest, he knelt on the bed and placed the tray between them.

Gina opened sleepy eyes. She blinked a few times, almost as if she didn't know where she was, then her beautiful blue eyes grew wide.

"Good morning," he said.

Her lips curved into a smile that was both sexy and shy. Justin wanted nothing more than to set the food aside and work up an appetite with this lady, starting with kissing her amazing mouth.

"Good morning," she replied, her gaze moving from him to the wooden tray. "Wow, what's all this?"

"Breakfast." Justin leaned back against the pillows. "Hope you're hungry."

Gina sat up, keeping the sheet tucked around her. "Oh, this is beautiful! You didn't have to do all this."

Her enthusiasm caused a shiver of pride to course through him. "I wanted to. So, what will it be first? Juice or coffee?"

"Juice, please."

He handed her a glass and took one of the mugs for himself. Gina reached for a pineapple flower, then stopped.

"You can eat them," Justin said, smiling. "That's why they're on the plate."

"But they're too pretty to eat."

Justin took a sip of coffee and returned the mug to the tray. He cut a piece of crepe with a fork and held it out to her. "Here, try this instead."

She accepted his offer, a dollop of whipped cream landing on her upper lip as she closed her mouth.

"You missed some." He swiped away the cream with his fingertip.

Gina swallowed, then her lips turned downward in a pretty pout. "You couldn't think of a better way to remove that? Here, let me show you."

She dipped one finger into the whipped cream, then trailed the cream over his chin before she lapped it away. "Hmm, much better."

And just like that, he wanted her.

Again.

Justin repeated her actions, only his target was a bit lower. Seconds later, he was leaving a damp path over the swell of her breasts until Gina pressed her hand to his cheek and guided his mouth up to hers for a deep kiss. Succumbing for several minutes before finally pulling away, he lunged off the bed and placed the tray on the dresser. Her giggle and the gleam in her eyes had him reaching for the top button on his jeans.

He'd released two when a loud knock came at his front door. "What the— Who could that be?"

Gina shook her head and the knocking came again. "Jacoby?"

"No, he's with Racy and Gage until after church services this morning. Wait here, I'll be right back."

She nodded and Justin walked into the living room, quickly redoing the buttons on his jeans. He made it to the door when the knocking started for a third time. Grabbing the handle, he twisted the lock and yanked the door open. Surprise filled him when he found both Leeann Harris and Gage standing on his front porch.

"What's going on? Is something wrong? Is Jacoby okay?"

At the mention of his son, the stranger Justin noticed standing next to Gage caught his breath.

"Justin, this gentleman is Richard Ellsworth," Gage said. "Jacoby's fine, but we need to talk."

Why did that name sound familiar? Justin gaze flew from the stranger to Gina's brother to Leeann. "Now?"

Leeann nodded. "Yes, now."

He pushed open the screen door and stepped back. He saw the sheriff department's Jeep parked between his ratty pickup and the vintage 1946 candy-apple-red Ford pickup he and Gina had used last night to get to the dance.

Gage's vintage 1946 candy-apple-red Ford pickup.

Having no idea what was going on or if Gina would stay out of sight, Justin motioned for his surprise guests to have a seat, thankful he'd cleaned up Gina's first-aid stuff from the coffee table this morning.

Grabbing a clean T-shirt from the laundry stacked on the dining room table and pulling it on, he noticed how interested Richard Ellsworth was in the cabin. His sharp gaze took in everything from the secondhand furniture to the mess Justin had left in the kitchen after fixing breakfast. He guessed the man was in his midsixties by the gray hair, and the tailored suit jacket, dress slacks, leather loafers and shiny gold watch told him he came from money.

Justin had just moved to the couch when the sound of a door opening caught everyone's attention.

Seconds later, Gina walked into the room.

Dressed in one of his flannel shirts and a baggy pair of sweats, she padded barefoot to Justin's side. The worry on her face caused him to smile as she placed a hand on his arm before offering a gentle hello to her brother and Leeann. Justin had to give them credit. Leeann's eyes widened for a moment before she schooled her features, and the good sheriff only offered a raised eyebrow.

"I'm sorry to interrupt," Gina said to everyone, "but I heard my brother's voice and thought something might be wrong."

Justin made a quick introduction while he tried again to figure out how he knew this man. "This is my— This is Gina Steele. Gina, this is Richard Ellsworth."

The man nodded from where he sat next to Leeann on the love seat, then spoke. "Ms. Steele, Mr. Dillon, let me get right to it. I'm Susan Ellsworth's father. I've been told you know her as Zoe Ellis."

Astonished, Justin sank to the couch, pulling Gina down beside him. As he gripped her hand, he flashed back to his conversation with Leeann about Zoe's car being found in Reno. He tried to connect the obviously wealthy man in front of him with the ragtag girl who'd walked out a month ago leaving her son—their son—behind.

Gina's touch warmed him as she covered their joined fingers with her other hand. He looked from her to Gage, and then to Leeann. "Does this mean you found her? You found Zoe, ah, Susan?"

Leeann nodded, but it was Richard Ellsworth who spoke.

"Yes, in a matter of speaking."

Justin looked at him again, closely this time, and saw how much he looked like Jacoby. He also saw anguish in the man's eyes.

"My daughter…" He paused and swallowed hard before continuing. "Susan is dead."

Chapter Thirteen

"Dead?"

Richard Ellsworth nodded, then dropped Justin's gaze and stared at his own clenched hands in his lap. "A car accident on a highway outside of Las Vegas. They identified her body with an expired driver's license and called us. She also had a picture of her—of a child in her pocket."

Justin tried to process what the man was saying, but confusion reigned. He looked to Gage and Leeann.

"That's how Mr. Ellsworth found out about his daughter's death," Leeann explained. "And about his grandson."

"My wife, Elizabeth, is devastated." Richard pulled in a deep breath before he continued, drawing Justin's attention back to him. "Susan was our only child. Growing up, she was so independent and creative. She loved to sing and draw, always talked about leaving our home in Boulder to go to Hollywood, to be in the movies. But by the time she was a teenager, she'd gotten involved with drugs and alcohol, skipping school and disappearing for days at a time."

His voice broke, but he kept talking. "We tried to help her, got her enrolled in a treatment program her senior year of high school, but as soon as she was eighteen she checked herself out and disappeared. We went to the police, hired private investigators, but she was gone. Until we got the call…"

The man reached into his jacket and withdrew the photograph. He held it out, but Justin couldn't move. It was as if he was frozen in place, until Gina nudged him to take it.

Worn with bent corners, the image showed a baby not even old enough to sit up yet, propped up against a blue blanket embellished with a baseball glove. With dark eyes and the familiar lopsided grin, Justin knew he was looking at his son.

"Elizabeth stayed at home to start making…arrangements. I plan to have Susan returned home as soon as the autopsy is complete." Richard ran his fingers through his hair. "When I found out someone was looking for her, and why, I came to Destiny. Deputy Harris filled me in on what Susan did last month by showing up here…"

Justin knew the man was still talking, but everything faded as he stared at Jacoby's picture.

His son. His family.

Jacoby, Racy and yes, even jailbird Billy Joe, were all the family Justin had in this world. But not Jacoby. His little boy had other people out there who shared his blood, his genes. People who cared about him. Grandparents. Why hadn't Zoe, ah, Susan, gone home when she needed help?

"Justin?"

Gina's voice broke into his thoughts and he realized the room was quiet. "I'm sorry. You were saying?"

"All these years, my wife and I never knew Susan had a child. Maybe if she'd come to us, we could've helped— would've had a chance to know our grand—" Richard Ellsworth stopped and cleared his throat. "I take it from your reaction when we arrived he isn't here?"

Justin shook his head.

"I see. The sheriff's report says Jacoby is seven years old. Do you have any recent pictures of him?"

He didn't. Justin looked around the living room, comparing it again with the numerous framed pictures he'd seen last night at the Steele family home.

Despite his attempts, this place still lacked a feeling of home and family. With the fire in January that had destroyed the house he'd grown up in, he had no mementos from his past; not that there'd been anything in that old place he would've wanted.

Racy had managed to save a box full of old family photos she kept at her office, many of which she'd framed and scattered around her and Gage's place, but he'd never thought to ask for any of them, not even the one of him and Racy with their mother taken shortly after Racy was born.

And in the month Jacoby had been with him, he'd never take a photograph of the boy.

"I have one." Gina rose from the couch and went into the kitchen for a moment. She returned with several pieces of paper and her sequined purse.

"I thought you might like to see these. Justin hangs Jacoby's artwork all over the fridge." She placed the drawings in Richard's outstretched hands. "As you can see, he's quite an artist."

Sitting back down, she reached into her purse and withdrew her cell phone. Justin watched as she flipped it open and brought up the image of Jacoby and Jack. His heart lodged in his throat, for a reason he couldn't explain, as she handed the phone to Jacoby's grandfather.

"This was taken just a few weeks ago," Gina said.

The man eagerly took the phone and gazed at the picture. "He has my wife's smile...Susan's smile. Is this his dog?"

"That's Jack, he belongs to my sister." Justin shifted his

attention to Gage for a moment. "That's where Jacoby is, spending the night."

Richard's gaze flickered between Justin and Gina before he spoke. "Is he due home soon? I'd like to meet him."

This time, it felt like his heart dropped to his feet before zooming back to its natural place. He fought against the urge to rub his fist against his chest in an attempt to lessen the erratic pounding. "Ah, that might not be a good idea—"

"He is my grandson," Richard interrupted.

"And he's my son."

"Are you sure? Given my daughter's behavior before she disappeared, you are probably one of many men she was involved with. From what I've read, you've only known about Jacoby for a month now."

The man had every right to ask the question and Justin refused to react to the sudden anger that flashed through his veins. Gina leaned into him, offering support with her warmth and soft curves. Silence filled the room as Justin held the man's gaze.

"Yes, I'm sure. I have the DNA results to prove it." He sat a bit taller and squared his shoulders. "I understand the last couple of days have been very traumatic for you and your wife, Mr. Ellsworth, and I'm sorry about that, but I will be the one to tell Jacoby about his mother and his grandparents."

Finally, Richard nodded. "It's going to be a few days before her body is released. We're holding services next weekend in Boulder. We would like for Jacoby—for the both of you—to be there."

Twelve days and they were finally home.

Gina's fingers tightened on the steering wheel as she headed for the cabin, remembering how Justin and Richard Ellsworth had exchanged phone numbers that Sunday morning in the cabin, then everyone left. She'd wanted to stick around, but Justin had already started to pull away from her, both physically and emotionally. When he'd asked for time alone, his voice so heartbreakingly sad and his goodbye kiss so tender, she'd gathered her things and drove home in Gage's truck.

Two days later, Justin and Jacoby left for Boulder and except for one quick call, she hadn't heard from them. He'd phoned Racy to let her know they'd arrived safely, except Gina had ended up intercepting his call because she'd been at her boss's desk. She'd heard the surprise in Justin's voice when she'd answered and he'd kept their conversation short. She'd asked about Jacoby and he'd said the boy was subdued but fine. When she asked him how he was doing, a long silence filled the air before he'd replied with the same answer and ended the call.

Now they were back.

Racy had handed her a take-out order when her shift ended, asking if she'd like to make a delivery. She'd glanced at the name. Justin.

Parking her car, she grabbed the bag and walked to the porch. She raised her hand to knock when the door swung open.

"I'm ready to go— Oh, hi, Gina!"

She looked down through the screen door at Jacoby dressed in his baseball uniform, the number two on the front of his jersey. "Hi, are you getting ready for a game?"

"Just practice. I'm waiting for Dustin's mom to pick me up." Jacoby pushed open the door. "You wanna come in?"

"Where's your dad—"

"Jacoby, did you say something—"

Justin stepped into the living room, pulling a denim shirt over his shoulders. He froze in the doorway and she was powerless to look away. He looked the same but different. There were lines around his eyes, like he hadn't slept well. Considering all that had happened she wasn't surprised, and she wanted nothing more than to go to him and wrap him in her arms.

Instead, she held up the bag of food. "I have your order from The Blue Creek. Delivery service complimentary."

"Ah, thanks," Justin said. "We just got back this afternoon and there's no food in the house."

"Come on in, Gina, I'm starved!"

She pulled her gaze from Justin and smiled at Jacoby. Entering the cabin, she set the bag on the dining room table and tried not to watch as Justin buttoned up his shirt, but it was impossible.

The last two weeks had been quiet and lonely without these two guys in her life. She missed seeing Jacoby at the library and stopping by the ball field to watch him play. And after that amazing night she and Justin had shared, she missed him, too.

"You're going to have to eat after practice," Justin said. "Unless you'd rather stay home tonight?"

"But I've missed a lot already 'cause of—'cause we went to Colorado." Jacoby turned to look at Gina. "I guess you know about my mom, huh?"

Gina dropped into one of the chairs at the table. "Yes, and I'm really sorry."

"We had to go to her funeral. There were a lot of people there." Jacoby shrugged. "I didn't know any of them except my dad. My mom…she was laying in this really fancy box with lots of flowers around her. She looked like she was sleeping, but I knew she really wasn't."

Gina willed away the sudden sting of tears. Her resolve was tested even more when Justin moved in behind his son and placed his hands on the boy's tiny shoulders.

"My dad didn't make me go up and look at her," the boy continued. "But I'm never going to get a chance to talk to her again. That stinks."

"I know what you mean. My daddy died when I was a

little girl and I still miss him very much." Gina glanced up at Justin, finding his gaze on her. She focused on Jacoby again. "But when I want to share something with him I still talk to him."

"Really? Do you think he hears you, even if he can't answer?"

"Yes, I'm sure of it." She nodded, watching as Jacoby seemed to think about what she said for a long moment.

"We stayed in a motel for a couple of days."

Surprised at the switch in topics, she went with it. "Was it a nice place?"

"Yeah, then we went to stay with my grandparents. They're my mom's mom and dad. They said they had plenty of room for us and, boy, do they ever! Their house is huge!" Jacoby spread his arms wide. "They have a ton of bedrooms and a three-car garage and a great big backyard with a swimming pool and it has a waterfall and jack-uzie."

"Jacuzzi," Justin cut in.

"Right, one of those things. The water gets really hot and there's lots of bubbles and— Oh, wait until you see this!" Jacoby pulled from his father's touch and raced to his bedroom. Seconds later he was back, pushing a shiny two-wheeled bike. "Isn't this cool?"

Gina looked from the bike to where Justin now stood at the kitchen counter, but his attention was on emptying the bag of food. "Wow, that's a nice bike."

"Grandpa Richard and Grandma Liz gave it to me. And guess what? I have another one just like it down at their house, so I can ride it when I go to visit."

Before Gina could think of a response, a car horn beeped.

"That's Dustin. I gotta go." Jacoby turned to his dad. "Can I leave this out here for now?"

Justin nodded. Jacoby put down the bike's kickstand and grabbed his baseball glove and duffel bag from the couch.

"Hey, hold on." Justin handed Jacoby a small cooler. "Your aunt Racy made your favorite sandwich and I added a couple of bottles of water."

"Thanks, Dad. Bye, Gina."

Gina waved goodbye. Justin walked Jacoby outside and helped him get into the already-crowded minivan. Justin watched the van drive away, and once it was out of sight, he went to his truck for a moment before coming back inside. Closing the door, he slumped against it, his posture one of hopelessness.

"Are you okay?"

He shook his head. "It's been a long couple of weeks for Jacoby."

"For the both of you." Gina rose, wanting to go to him, but unsure if she should. "Jacoby seems to be handling things okay."

"Because the Ellsworths made it so easy for him while we were there." Justin sighed, slapping the manila envelope in his hand against his leg. "And so damn hard for me."

"For you— What are you talking about? What happened?"

"When we were ready to leave, Liz Ellsworth was getting Jacoby settled in the truck, while Richard pulled me into his office. He said he wanted to talk…about Jacoby's fu-future—"

As his voice broke, she crossed the room and wrapped him in her arms. Justin stood as if frozen in place, but she only held him tighter, wishing she could ease whatever burden he was carrying.

He finally relented and leaned into her, holding her close for a moment. Then he reached up and unhooked her arms and stepped away. "Look, I appreciate you bringing the food, but I've got a lot to do—"

"What happened, Justin?"

He returned her stare for a long moment, then handed her

the envelope before he walked across the room. Gina opened the envelope and pulled out folded paperwork, recognizing it as a legal document. She started to read the opening paragraph, but shock at the words stopped her.

"What is this?"

Justin ignored her question as he went back to dividing up the take-out order into plastic containers.

"Justin?"

He finally stilled. Looking at her, his dark eyes held that familiar unreadable emotion she'd seen before. "The Ellsworths want custody of Jacoby."

"What?" A silent scream rose from deep inside her. Her fingers clenched the document. "I can't believe this. What are you going to do?"

Justin remained silent.

"You're not thinking of agreeing, are you?"

"They're good people." He rounded the counter and came back into the living room. "And they're the kid's grandparents. Their daughter raised Jacoby for seven years—"

"And did such a great job she decided to walk out on him and leave someone she barely knew to pick up the pieces!"

"I've only been in the kid's life a month."

"And in that time you've proven you're capable of taking care of Jacoby." She tossed the paperwork onto the table. "Look at all you've given him—"

"Clothes from a discount store and a secondhand bed." He waved a hand toward Jacoby's bedroom. "I'm not talking about those things. My father made sure I had the basics and no one would vote him Father of the Year."

She heard the conviction behind his words. "You're not your father."

"I was raised by a man who took a belt to us, who berated my siblings and me with cruel and belittling words whenever the mood struck him. How do I know I won't turn out to be the same?"

Justin paced the length of the room. "It hasn't been all baking cookies and reading stories around here. Jacoby's struggling in school. He's behind the other kids in everything from reading to math. He gets angry and frustrated and he's starting to act out. And all of that was before he found out about his mother."

Gina had noticed Jacoby's refusal to participate in the library story hour when the children read a few pages aloud. "It's tough being the new kid in school. Maybe he just needs more time to adjust."

"It's more than that." Justin dropped his voice to a low whisper as he jammed his hands into the pockets of his jeans. "I mentioned his nightmares before. Well, they haven't stopped. The first time it…it scared the hell out of me when I realized he wasn't really awake, just sort of stuck between what was going on inside his head and consciousness."

"Oh, that's terrible."

"His eyes are open but vacant, and he's crying…crying for his mother."

The pain in his voice, the defeat in his hunched shoulders was too much for Gina. She went to him, placing her hand on his arm. "And you help him through that."

"I talk to him, calm him down, and eventually he goes back to sleep. The first night I sat in the corner of his room and watched him until the sun came up. When I try to bring up what happened the next day, he claims he doesn't remember what he dreamed about." Justin backed away and went to the counter. He braced his hands there, his back to her. "But to hear him…crying out for her and now she's gone…"

Fear seized her in a viselike grip. "And you think the Ellsworths can fill that void better than you?"

"Gina, look at the differences between us." He turned back to her. "I live in a two-bedroom shack owned by my brother-in-law. I work in a bar with my hours cut because I need to be here at night. Thankfully, my sister is paying me enough so I'm getting by, barely. My truck is almost to the legal drinking age and ready to fall apart."

It broke her heart to hear him talk that way. "Justin, you're not giving yourself a chance. The cabin is beautiful with all the work you've put into it. Jacoby's mother grew up in a mansion and look how she turned out. It's not about where you live but making a child feel loved and safe and cared for."

An idea popped into her head. "And who says you have to continue working at the bar. You have a college degree and you were fantastic with those kids at the dance. You could teach."

"What kind of fantasy world do you live in, Gina? I got that degree while in prison for drug trafficking. Do you really think the school board is going to allow someone like me to teach their kids?"

"But you were great at the dance! Talking about what you've learned from past mistakes, not to mention you put yourself in harm's way to protect those kids."

She had to make him see there was so much more to him than his past. That he could have a future with his son and maybe even with her, if he would just believe in himself.

"You're wonderful with Jacoby. I know it's been hard since he came into your life, but please don't demean what you've accomplished. You're a good man, Justin. Your son needs to be with you and you need to be with him."

"What I need doesn't matter anymore. The moment that boy came into my life, my wants and needs ceased to be important. I've been a selfish, self-centered person most of my life, always looking out for number one." His words were passionate, but his face expressionless, his eyes cold and life-less. "That's not who I am anymore. I have to put what Jacoby wants and needs before anything else."

He'd already made up his mind.

For a long moment Gina could do nothing but stand there,

utterly still, as if an icy shower had splashed over her. It seeped into every crack and crevice until it reached her heart. The pain numbed her from the inside out until it felt like she was made of glass, ready to shatter if he uttered one more word.

"Well, I'll leave you alone to make your own decision."

He blinked, as if her words woke him from a trance. "Gina, I'm sorry, but you don't understand…"

She closed her eyes.

Justin was right. Who was she to tell him what he needed? Because she loved him and his little boy?

Yes, she loved Jacoby.

She loved him as much as she loved his father. And she couldn't stick around and watch Justin throw it all away. "I do understand, Justin, more than you could possibly know."

A week later, Gina answered the knock at her front door, knowing it was Racy. "Thanks for coming by so quickly after I called— Ah, hi, Jacoby."

"Gina!" Toting his raggedy pillow case, the little boy entered and gave her a big hug.

"I didn't know you'd be here," she said.

"Sorry about this," Racy said, following her nephew inside. "I'd just picked him up at school when you called."

"Yeah, my dad has an appointment, so I'm hanging out with my aunt Racy," Jacoby said. "Cool, huh?"

"Very cool," Gina agreed, forcing her smile to stay in place.

An appointment? It had to be with the Ellsworths.

A sharp pain jabbed at her heart, and she tried not to respond. She'd thought she'd accepted this physical reaction that happened every time she thought about Justin. Maybe someday it would fade, but for now, she needed to let go of wanting to help him live his life.

It was past time she focus on her own life.

"You sounded like you really wanted to talk," Racy added, "so I thought I'd stop by and tell you it'll probably be until after dinner tonight before we can hook up."

Garrett entered from the kitchen. "Hey, Racy," he said around a mouthful of chips. "Hey, squirt. What are you two doing here?"

"They stopped by for a visit." Gina eyed the junk food. "Aren't you supposed to be studying for finals?"

"Taking a break for a nutritional refill," Garrett said, then turned to Jacoby. "You ever play Space Blaster 9000?"

Jacoby shook his head.

"You're in luck. I'm about ready to crack the galactic warrior level." He headed for the stairs. "Come with me."

The boy looked at Gina. "Can I?"

Racy nodded, so Gina said, "Sure, if you want."

Jacoby raced after her brother, catching up with him at the first step. "What are they going to do?"

"Girl talk, probably." Garrett handed off a soda can to Jacoby as they made their way to the second floor. "You know, makeup, nails, clothes, that kind of stuff."

Gina tried not to laugh at the way Jacoby scrunched up his nose at her brother's words. She looked at Racy and found her with a wide smile.

"Garrett is so like Gage," Racy said. "But that was a sweet thing to do. So, I guess we can have that chat now, even though I'm still not happy about you quitting on me so suddenly last weekend."

Gina's smiled disappeared. "I'm sorry about that, but I just couldn't—"

"Hey, it's okay." Racy gave her arm a quick squeeze. "I was just teasing. The other girls are happy to pick up your hours."

"Why don't we go up to my room and talk?" Gina said. "Maybe I can explain things a little better?"

Racy nodded and Gina headed up the stairs. Once they

were inside her room, she kicked the door closed, then flopped down on her bed.

"Wow, is it that bad?" Racy dropped her purse to the floor and sat next to her. "What's my brother done now?"

Gina stared at the ceiling, knowing if she even looked at her sister-in-law the tears would start. "What makes you think Justin has anything to do with this?"

"You've been attracted to him from the first day you met, you shocked the family, not to mention the entire town, by having a sleepover at his apartment—" Racy ticked off reasons with one hand "—you've been playing that 'I like you, I hate you' flirt game for months, something I am a pro at, by the way, just ask Gage. You've been helping him adjust to fatherhood, your first date including a knife fight and another sleepover—"

Gina turned to Racy.

"Yes, everyone knows, and believe me, your mother and I have had our hands full insisting Gage respect your privacy about that night. Then Justin drops the bomb about Jacoby's other family and disappears for almost two weeks, he returns and twenty-four hours later you quit your job, having decided waitressing just isn't for you." Racy paused and blew out a deep breath. "Whew! How could Justin not be involved?"

Gina sighed and looked back at the ceiling again. "Okay, you win. I'm in love with your brother."

"Boy, you get to the heart of a heart-to-heart pretty fast." Racy reached out and grabbed her hand. "Does my brother love you, too?"

"No."

"How do you know?"

Gina sat up and brushed at her face, getting rid of the tears. Then she told Racy everything—well, maybe not everything—that had happened between her and Justin over the last month, ending with her recent decision to make some changes in her life.

"Like quitting The Blue Creek?" Racy asked.

"Like leaving town," Gina replied.

Chapter Fourteen

"What?"

Gina realized she could've put that more tactfully. "I've decided to go back to school. To get my teaching credentials," she continued, sitting forward on the bed, a surge of excitement filling her as she spoke her plan aloud for the first time. "I love working with the kids at the library. It's fueled my desire to teach at the elementary school level."

"That's great. I've seen you during those story hours and I can tell you love it, but why do you have to leave town?" Racy asked. "Can't you take classes at the University of Wyoming?"

Gina stood and walked to her dresser, mindlessly playing with her combs and hair clips. When her fingers inched toward the dried-up corsage sitting atop her jewelry box, she clenched her hands together.

Jacoby had handed her a brown lunch bag after a story hour last week saying it belonged to her. Inside was the corsage. No note, nothing but the dried flowers.

"I can't stay in Destiny and not be— It would just hurt too much to see…"

"Justin?"

"And Jacoby." Gina turned to face her sister-in-law again. "He is the sweetest boy and I love him to pieces. I know Justin is running scared at the moment, but deep down I believe he's going to do the right thing for himself and his son."

"The right thing?"

"Finding out about Jacoby's mother and the Ellsworths has got Justin all twisted. He doubts his ability to raise Jacoby."

"Do you— Did he tell you what the Ellsworths want?"

Gina nodded.

"I guess you've figured out Richard Ellsworth is in town again and Justin's talking with him right now."

Not trusting her voice, Gina again nodded.

"I've tried to get him to talk to me about this. I know he feels like he's been handling things with Jacoby on a wing and a prayer. I'd hoped once he knew for sure Jacoby was his that would change." Racy sighed. "Maybe it's just made it harder for him because of the way we were raised."

"He's so scared he's going to turn into your father."

"As crazy as it sounds, I understand his fears. My dad was abusive, both verbally and physically. I don't know how many times Justin stepped in front of me…" Racy paused and swallowed hard "…protecting me from our father's brand of discipline. Billy Joe turned out to be just like him. It was me and Justin against the two of them. So many times he took what both of them dished out so I…I wouldn't have to."

Gina sat back down on her bed and hugged Racy hard. Having been raised in a strict but always loving family, she couldn't fathom what her sister-in-law described.

Racy returned her hug, then pulled back and brushed tears from her face. "Maybe what Justin needs is professional help. I think I'll suggest that tonight when he comes to dinner. Of course, what he really needs is a good lawyer so he can fight for his son."

Gina thought both were great ideas. Not that coming to terms with his childhood would do anything to solve what was, or wasn't, happening between them, but making things right between father and son was the most important thing at the moment.

"When I was working toward my degree I spent time with a counselor," Racy continued. "She helped me so much. Like Justin, I never thought I'd have children of my own. I was so scared I'd repeat the same horrible mistakes my father did."

"But you worked through it, right? Aren't you and Gage planning on having a family someday?"

Racy offered a wobbly smile. "Maybe sooner than you think."

"What?"

"Nothing. We were talking about you and Justin."

"There is no me and Justin. My head knows that. My heart is going to take a bit longer to catch up."

The words came so easy that Gina almost believed them.

Pushing her own issues aside for the moment, she focused on her sister-in-law. "Now, what aren't you telling me?"

Racy pulled her oversize purse to her lap, took out a paper bag and offered it to Gina.

"What's this?" Gina peeked inside. "A home pregnancy test?"

"Five tests, actually. I went to a group of drugstores in Laramie." Racy shrugged. "I wanted to cover my bases, in case one of them is a dud."

Gina let go of her worries for now and rejoiced in the exciting news. "Racy, this is wonderful! Does my brother know?"

"Not yet. Can you imagine if I bought these tests in town?

News of a Steele baby would spread so fast they'd be betting on the arrival date before I'd even had a chance to tell Gage."

Gina sighed, easily picturing her big, strong brother cradling a newborn in his arms. "He is going to be over the moon about being a daddy."

"I hope so." A sudden smile lit up Racy's face. "Let's do the test now."

"Now?"

"Sure, we could use the distraction." Racy rose from the bed and headed toward Gina's bathroom. "I'll be right back."

A few minutes later, Racy emerged with her eyes trained on her watch. "Okay, I replaced the caps to cover the absorbent tips, yuck, and I've set my alarm. We need to wait at least five minutes, but no more than ten."

Gina grinned. "Did you do all of them?"

Racy nodded and returned her smile. "Just to be safe."

Time seemed to crawl as Gina and Racy waited. When Racy's watch beeped, both women jumped.

Silencing the alarm, Racy glanced at the bathroom door. "I can't look."

"What? Why?"

"I thought I'd be okay no matter the results, but now..."

Gina squeezed Racy's hand. "You want me to check?"

Racy nodded.

Gina entered her bathroom and eyed the five testers on her sink. The results were identical. She took the first stick and headed back into her room.

"Yeah! We have a baby on the way!"

Justin stood at the oversize window in his sister's dining room. It looked out over a large yard surrounded by trees on three sides and Echo Lake on the fourth. The sun was just about gone, but it was another warm spring evening.

He'd shown up at Racy and Gage's home in time to join everyone for dinner. Now that the meal was over, Racy and Maggie Stevens, one of his sister's best friends, were in the kitchen cleaning up. Gage and Landon, Maggie's husband of a few months, had disappeared in the garage to check out Gage's new motorcycle.

Justin had waved off Gage's offer to join them and instead watched Jacoby race around the yard, playing man in the middle, or more appropriately dog in the middle, with Anna, Maggie's daughter. Jack, his sister's golden retriever, was trying his best to get the ball the kids tossed back and forth to each other.

We want our grandson. We can provide him with a stable life filled with the best of everything.

Richard Ellsworth's words, spoken during their meeting this afternoon, echoed in Justin's head. The big house, private schools and summer vacations around the world. It all sounded perfect. Perfect for a little boy with loving grandparents.

There was no way Justin could compete. He wasn't even sure he had the right to, even with the shift in people's attitudes toward him lately.

During the two days before they left for Colorado and in the week since they'd been back, he'd been thanked numerous times for stopping the fight at the school dance, by adults and teenagers, whenever he ventured from the kitchen into the bar's dining area or when out in town. He had to admit that when he'd told Jacoby why people were asking to shake his hand and offering their appreciation, it felt good when his son jumped into his arms and called him a hero.

But it couldn't erase all he'd done in his past.

Richard Ellsworth hadn't threatened outright to use his family history or prison record against him if it came down to a legal battle, but he made it clear that the court would do an extensive background check on all the parties involved.

He sighed and turned from the window, seeing his sister and Maggie had moved into the living room. Both women looked at him with expectant gazes.

"Do you want to tell us what happened today?" Racy asked.

"No."

The one he really wanted to talk to was Gina, but after the way she walked out on him last week, and made herself scarce ever since, he doubted she'd be willing to listen to anything he had to say.

His sister tilted her head and Justin knew he wasn't going to get out of this. He joined them, sitting on the end of couch. "I really don't want to talk about this."

"You need to," Racy persisted, "and you need to let your family and friends help."

"That includes me and Landon, too," Maggie added when Justin looked at her.

Racy leaned forward. "So, how did it go with Richard Ellsworth?"

Justin gave in and told his sister and Maggie everything, from what it was like staying with the Ellsworths following the funeral, to the day Richard gave him the custody papers and the details of what they'd talked about today, minus the obscure warning about his past.

"So, now I'm trying to figure out if I should pack up Jacoby's things." Justin rose, unable to sit still any longer. He paced the area in front of the fireplace. "I've been doing a lot of soul searching since we got back from Colorado, but the bottom line is the Ellsworths can give him all the things in life I can't."

"You're a great father," Racy said. "And they're damn lucky you are in light of the way their daughter just introduced you and Jacoby and then took off. To decide now they can raise him better—"

"They didn't know Jacoby existed."

"And that makes it okay?"

Justin sighed, crossed his arms over his chest. "I don't know what's okay anymore."

"You're not our father." Racy's voice was soft. "You would never raise a hand to your son."

He turned to look at his sister. "I've been thinking about that, too—Dad, our childhood—over the last week. Deep inside, I know I'm not like him. Having Jacoby in my life has made it confusing and frustrating at times, but I've never felt anything close to anger toward him."

"So why are you thinking about sending him away?" Maggie asked.

"Because I want to do what's best for him. Richard and Elizabeth can provide him with a loving and stable home—"

"So can you! Jacoby has family here, too." Racy stood. "Gage and I love him to pieces and he's already calling Gage's mom Nana Steele."

That surprised him. "He is?"

"Justin, I hope I'm not overstepping my bounds, but I know how important grandparents, or great-grandparents, can be in a child's life," Maggie spoke up. "I'm thankful every day that Nana B. found me and is here for Anna. She's a wonderful influence and has helped me tremendously in raising my daughter. Being a single parent is hard, but you aren't alone. We are all here to help and the Ellsworths can, too, as his grandparents."

"Do you love Jacoby?" Racy asked.

"More than my own life," Justin replied without hesitation.

"Do you want him to stay?"

He placed his hands on his hips, pulled in a deep breath and went with what was in his heart. "Yes, but—"

The sound of Maggie's daughter calling for her mom had

him cutting off his words. The little girl raced up the stairs from the lower level, a frown on her face.

"What's wrong, honey?" Maggie asked.

"Is Jacoby up here? We were playing hide-and-seek and he told me to count to two hundred because he had a really good hiding spot, but I've been looking and looking and I can't find him."

Alarm crawled into Justin's throat, making it impossible to speak. Gut instinct told him this wasn't good.

Stay calm. Just stay calm.

Maggie looked at her daughter. "When did you last see him?"

"A while ago," Anna said. "When we came inside to go to the bathroom."

"Isn't Jack with him?" Racy asked.

"Nope. He kept giving away our hiding spots, so we put him inside. He's lying under the pool table."

Justin swung around to look out the windows. The sun was gone and it was growing darker by the minute. He looked at his watch. Had he really been talking for forty-five minutes?

Talking— Dammit, had Jacoby overheard their conversation?

"We'll all look for him." Racy stood. "Justin, check with Gage and Landon. Maybe Jacoby is with them looking at the motorcycle."

A silent prayer winged its way heavenward as Justin headed for the stairs. He burst into the garage, his stomach dropping to his feet at finding only the two men there. He quickly relayed what had happened. Gage grabbed a couple of flashlights from a nearby workbench. The three men went outside to search the woods while the women searched the house.

Justin stomped through the woods calling out his son's name, but all he heard was Gage and Landon doing the same.

There was no sign of Jacoby. They met back at the stone patio outside the lower-level family room.

"Where the hell could he be?" Justin spat out the words, shoving the panic down hard into his gut. "Where could he have gone?"

"His pillowcase is missing," Racy said, stepping outside to join them. "He left it near the front door when we came in."

Locking his knees to keep himself standing, Justin pulled in a deep breath through his nose.

Jacoby had run away. But where? And why?

"Okay, this is what we're going to do," Gage spoke with quiet authority. "Maggie will stay here with Anna in case he comes back. Justin, go to the cabin. Maybe he went there. Racy, Landon and I will take separate vehicles and check in town, covering the diner, the library and the playgrounds."

"Do you really think he's made it to town?" Landon asked.

"It's been roughly thirty minutes since Anna last saw him, closer to an hour since Justin watched the kids through the window," Gage said. "We'll meet at my office. If anyone finds him, call me, and I'll call Justin."

Landon and Racy left, but Justin grabbed hold of Gage. "You haven't asked me about my meeting with Richard Ellsworth."

"I figured we'd talk about that after Maggie and Landon headed home. Do you think he might have something to do with Jacoby taking off? Does Jacoby know they want custody of him?"

"He might have overheard us talking about it."

Justin told his brother-in-law what he'd shared with Racy and Maggie. "I thought the kids were still outside, but maybe Jacoby came back in and heard me."

"And he's gone to find him?"

The thought of his little boy out in the dark was killing

him. That he might be trying to get to his grandfather made him feel like someone had ripped open his chest and torn out his heart. "I don't know. Should I check at the Destiny Inn, too?"

"Not yet. Chances are Jacoby hasn't gotten that far, but I'll cover that end of town. We don't want to give Ellsworth any reason to doubt your ability to care for your son."

"Any more than I doubt it myself?"

"Don't worry." Gage clapped him on the back. "We'll find him."

Justin raced to his truck and headed home. The cabin was dark, but he forced himself to go inside and check anyway. No Jacoby, but there was something missing. The new bike. He got back in his truck and headed into town, calling Gage in the process.

"He wasn't at the cabin," he said when his brother-in-law answered. "But the bike and helmet the Ellsworths gave him are gone. He must've come back for it."

"Racy and Landon are still looking. I'll head for the inn," Gage replied. "Racy said you might want to check my mother's house next."

"Your mother's?"

"I guess Racy and Jacoby were there earlier today visiting Gina. Your boy seems quite attached to my sister."

"Would he even remember how to get there?" Justin asked.

"In a town the size of Destiny? Besides, he could ask anyone for directions."

Justin remained silent.

"Hello?"

"Ah, yeah, you're right. Jacoby really likes Gina." Justin pushed the words past his dry throat. "I'll go there now."

He tried to call Gina's cell phone, but she didn't pick up. Moments later, he pulled up to the curb and raced to the front porch. He knocked loudly and waited.

Gina opened the door, surprise on her face. "Justin?"

He could already tell but he asked anyway. "Is Jacoby here?"

"No, why would you think—"

"He's run away."

His words changed the surprise on her face to shock and she reached for him. Justin backed away. He couldn't let her touch him. If she did, he'd shatter into a million pieces.

"Please, come in." She stepped back and opened the door wider.

"I can't." He started to back off the porch. "I need—I need to find him."

"Let me help," she said. "I'll go with you."

He stopped. "You don't have to do that."

Gina grabbed a jacket off a nearby hook and stepped across the threshold. "Of course I do."

"Hey, sis," Garrett appeared at the door as Gina started to close it. "Did I hear you say Jacoby's missing?"

Gina and Justin turned in unison. "Do you know anything?" Justin asked.

Garrett shrugged. "It might be nothing, but I was just in the kitchen and I thought I saw a flash of light coming from the tree house in the backyard."

Gina went back inside and Justin was right behind her as they crossed the living room and headed for the dark kitchen.

"How would Jacoby know about the tree house?" Gina asked.

"I told him," Garrett said, joining them at the back door. "See? Right there."

Justin saw the quick beam of light reflecting off the newly budded tree branches. He reached for the doorknob, but Gina stopped him, covering his hand with hers. His skin tingled with awareness at her touch, and they both sprang apart.

"L-let me go first." Gina's voice came out a shaky whisper. "We don't want to scare him, if it is him."

Justin nodded and stepped back.

Gina went outside first, crossed the large back deck and hurried down the steps to the grass. The tree house was among a cluster of trees in the corner of the yard. She reached the wooden ladder that rested against the base of the tree, then turned and waved at him.

His heart in his throat, Justin bolted from the house and was by her side seconds later. She placed her fingers to her lips and started to climb the ladder.

"Hey, there," she said when she reached the top, her head and shoulders now inside the wooden structure. "Do you have the secret password to be in the Steele family tree house?"

Justin held his breath. Then he watched as she maneuvered one hand back down to her side and gave him the thumbs-up sign. Slumping against the rough bark of the tree, he pressed his fingertips hard against his closed eyes.

Jacoby was up there.

He wiped at the wetness on his face and dug out his cell phone. Stepping away, he called Gage and passed along the news, catching him before he pulled into the inn's parking lot. Gage promised to let Racy and Landon know.

Justin ended the call and moved back to the ladder, listening to Gina talk to his son. He couldn't make out her words, but her love and concern for the boy were evident.

From the first moment she'd met Jacoby, she'd always put his needs and wants first, whether it was making sure he washed his hands or finding out the real reason he was scared to sleep in his new bed.

How could he have accused her of not understanding—

He looked up when the ladder creaked. Gina started to climb down and his hands itched to circle her waist to guide her to the ground, but he doubted Gina would welcome his touch.

Not anymore.

She stepped off the last rung and turned to him. "He'll talk to you now."

"I don't know what to say to him."

"Yes, you do." Gina laid her hand on his chest. "Just listen to him and tell him what's in your heart."

Justin clenched his hands into fists to keep from reaching for her. He settled instead for the warmth of her touch through his shirt before she suddenly dropped her hand and stepped away.

He climbed the ladder, his shoulders a tight squeeze as he made his way through the opening. He found his son sitting in the far corner on a sleeping bag, his pillowcase at his feet and his teddy bear clutched to his chest.

"Jacoby? Can I come in?"

Chapter Fifteen

Jacoby hoped his dad wasn't mad.

He didn't look mad. He looked worried.

Just like Gina said.

Jacoby nodded and watched his dad climb inside, hitting his head on the ceiling as he sat, bow-legged, the tree house too short for his long legs.

"Are you okay?" his dad asked. "You're not hurt?"

Jacoby looked down at his bear and shook his head.

"You know, you've got a lot of people worried about you."

He nodded.

"Your uncle Gage, aunt Racy and Landon, Anna's step-daddy, and I have been looking all over town for you."

Jacoby nodded again. Gina had already told him all this, but he figured his dad was going to say it, too. He knew it was wrong to run away, but he didn't know what else to do.

He hadn't planned to go that far, just hide until *he* left

town. If his dad still didn't want him after that, and Jacoby figured he didn't, he'd find someplace else to live.

"I was worried about you."

The soft way his dad spoke made him look up.

Did he mean it? If he did, why did he want him to go live with his grandparents?

"When I realized you'd left Aunt Racy's house I...I got really scared. Scared I'd never see you again."

"It's not fun to be scared."

Justin shook his head. "No, not fun at all."

"Is that why you want me to go live with them? Grandpa Richard and Grandma Liz? So you won't have to be scared about me anymore?"

Justin shifted closer. "I think I'll always be a little scared when you're out of my sight, even when you're all grown up."

Wow. "Why?"

"Because you're my son." Justin ruffled Jacoby's hair. "I love you and I want you to stay."

"You do?"

"Very much, but I also need to do what's best for you. I know it's been a little rough for you being here with me. Those nightmares you've been having must be scary, too."

Jacoby nodded. "I don't like 'em."

"Maybe they'd go away if you talked to someone about them."

"Like you?"

Justin nodded. "Sure, or maybe we could ask your doctor if he knows anyone who might help you feel better."

"Okay, but I don't want to live with Grandpa Richard and Grandma Liz. Their house is cool, but please don't make me leave," Jacoby pleaded. "I mean, I like 'em, but I love my school. I'll do better, I swear. And I love my baseball team. I even caught a fly ball for the first time this week and I love my room now. It's not scary at all. And Daddy, I love you. Most of all."

His dad scrubbed a hand across his mouth, then spread his arms wide. "Come here, son."

Jacoby launched himself at his father. His dad squeezed him tight and it felt good. Felt safe. Like nothing and no one would ever hurt him again.

He always thought crying was for sissies, but his dad had said it was okay to cry if he wanted to. He'd thought he'd used all his tears when he learned about his mom, but he couldn't stop his eyes from getting wet.

He buried his face in his father's shirt. "I know my mom didn't want me and then I thought you didn't want me anymore either. Please say I can stay. I'll be good, I promise. I think Gina is super and I'll even play nice with the new baby."

Justin stilled.

His unhinged panic at finding Jacoby safe had abated, but with one single word the emotion was back, pounding at his temple as he tried to absorb what Jacoby said.

Baby? Did he hear correctly? Had Jacoby said Gina was pregnant?

He leaned back to look at his son. "A baby?"

Jacoby nodded. "And I don't care if it's a baby brother or sister. I'll share all my toys. Except Clem." He hugged his bear tight. "He's mine."

Justin still couldn't wrap his mind around the idea.

Gina pregnant? It was impossible.

Okay, it wasn't impossible. It'd only been a little over two weeks since their night together. Justin's mind flew back to the first time they'd made love and twice more when they'd reached for each other during the night. He was sure he'd take the time—*each time*—to protect them both.

Pregnant?

"You still want me, don'tcha, Dad?"

The uncertainty in his son's voice pulled Justin from the memory. "Of course I want you. I love you, Jacoby." He hugged him close, rubbing his back until the boy relaxed against him. "And I'll do whatever it takes to keep you with me."

Whatever it takes.

Justin realized he needed a lot of help, most of it legal. He had no idea what it took to maintain physical custody of his son, but he was going to find out first thing in the morning.

But right now, he had to talk to Gina. Had to find out why she didn't tell him—

He placed one finger beneath Jacoby's chin and gently pressed so the boy would look at him. "Hey, how did you find out the bab—about Gina?"

Justin's eyes had adjusted to the dark so it was easy to read the guilty expression on the boy's face.

"I heard her tell Aunt Racy today. They were talking in Gina's bedroom."

"Maybe they were just talking about babies in general."

Jacoby shook his head and crawled off Justin's lap. He rooted around inside his pillowcase for a moment. Then he pulled something out.

Justin took the item from Jacoby's outstretched hand, turning the plastic piece over in his hands. "What's this?"

Jacoby grabbed the flashlight. Before he could shine it on the object, an outside light, probably from the back deck, lit the inside of the tree house, allowing Justin to see what he was holding.

A home pregnancy test. With a positive result.

Talk about a kick to the gut. Why hadn't Gina said anything to him about the possibility they might've created a baby together? She must've suspected something, otherwise she wouldn't have bought the test.

"Where did you get this?"

"From Gina's bathroom. After she told Aunt Racy about the baby. I found it on the floor, behind the garbage can."

She'd thrown it away? Why would she do that? Wait—

"How do you know what this is?" Justin waved the test stick in the air.

"My mom used to take them all the time."

"Why did you keep it instead of throwing it away?"

"My mom said it was proof that she was telling the truth." Jacoby shrugged. "Not that Gina lies."

She hadn't told the truth yet, either.

Justin tucked the stick in his jacket pocket. Then he sucked in a shallow breath, the best he could do at the moment, and let it out with a loud whoosh.

"So, what do you say we head home? It's past your bedtime and you've got school tomorrow."

"Are you going to tell Gina I told you?"

If she doesn't come to me first. "When I get the chance to talk to her, she'll probably want to know where I heard…" His voice faded as a thought sprang to his mind. "Did she— Was Gina upset? About the baby?"

"No, she sounded really excited."

Excited?

Justin wanted desperately to look out one of the small windows of the tree house to see if Gina was still standing in the yard. It was quiet, so he guessed she'd gone back inside to give him and Jacoby some privacy.

How was he going to look at her and not ask her the truth?

"Dad? Are we going now?"

"Sure, come on."

Justin left first because he was right in front of the door-way. Reaching the ground, he helped Jacoby, taking the pil-lowcase but allowing him to hold on to his stuffed bear. Once Jacoby was safely off the ladder, Justin noticed they weren't alone.

Racy and Gage stood silently on the deck with Gage's mother. Giselle was sitting at a nearby picnic table with Garrett perched on the top, his feet braced on the bench next to his twin.

And Gina was there, standing on the far side of the yard in the shadows.

His shock must've shown on his face as Racy hurried down the steps and came to him. "When you called Gage, we rushed right here," she said as if she had to explain their presence. "Landon went back to our place to tell Maggie the news. Is everything okay?"

"Ah, yeah, everything is fine." Justin forced his gaze away from Gina to look at his sister. "Everything is great, actually. Jacoby wants to stay with me, and I want that, too."

Cheers and clapping filled the air. Racy bent down and wrapped Jacoby in a big hug. Gage joined them and with everyone chatting at once, Justin slipped away to cross the yard.

"I want to talk to you," he said to Gina, his voice low.

She avoided looking at him as she took a half step back. "I think we're all talked out, but that's wonderful news about you and Jacoby."

He moved closer, invading her personal space. Keeping his back to everyone, he bent his head close to hers, his lips in the crown of her hair. "You know we need to talk."

"You made it quite clear you're not interested in anything I have to say." Gina's whispered reply blew hot on his neck. "We don't have anything more to say to each other."

She took another step and pushed at her hair, long and sleek this evening, moving it past one shoulder. That damn streak of pink caught and held his attention.

His insides twisted at the thought she was deliberately keeping the news of their child from him. Common sense told him this was the wrong place, the wrong time. Hell, she just took the test this afternoon, but he couldn't leave it alone. Not until she told him the truth.

"Gina, it's important—"

"So what's the next step? Where do you go from here?"

Racy's questions caused Justin to turn around. He faced everyone but stood angled next to Gina. If she tried to back away again she'd do it right into him.

"Aren't you going to have to talk to...?" His sister continued, inclining her head toward Jacoby, who was now sitting next to Garrett on the top of the picnic table.

Justin nodded, his mind zooming in twenty different directions. She was referring to the Ellsworths. Yes, he needed to talk to them, but first things first. "Yeah, but I need to get myself a lawyer first. Tomorrow if possible."

"We can help with that," Gage said with a grin. "Our cousin Jennifer is a lawyer in Laramie. Her specialty is family law. If her schedule is full I'm sure she can recommend someone in her firm you can meet with right away."

"And if you need someone to watch Jacoby, I'm available," Giselle offered. "And I'll even give up my usual hourly rate."

"Nah, the squirt is going to want to hang with me," Garrett said, reaching out to tickle Jacoby. "He needs to work on his skills at Space Blaster, huh?"

Jacoby laughed and wiggled from Garrett's grasp. "No, the first thing we gotta do is get married! My dad and Gina are gonna have a baby!"

Silence fell over the yard.

A dull buzzing zoned in Gina's ears. Her vision tunneled until everything around her was a hazy blur. All she saw was the little boy beaming at her with a goofy grin on his face and joy in his eyes.

Eyes so much like his father's.

She whirled to find Justin staring at her, too, only his eyes were somber and serious.

When he'd come to her after announcing he would fight for Jacoby, Gina had fought to keep her feet planted in the cool grass. With every step he took, she wanted to back away. Wanted to kick herself for the way her body reacted to the sight of him, looking impossibly sexy in faded jeans and black collared polo shirt with the Blue Creek logo over his heart. Wanted to smooth the brown locks standing on end, knowing he must've been tearing his hair out until Jacoby was found. Wanted to fly into his arms the moment he spoke, but proud that she'd managed to declare she wasn't interested in anything he had to say.

"What did he just say?" Gage's tone was hard, the kindness gone from his face as he marched from the deck, heading straight for Gina.

No, he was gunning for Justin.

She held out her hand to stop him. "I'm not pregnant."

"Sure you are!" Jacoby crowed.

"Gina, it's okay. I know." A warm hand cupped her elbow. She looked back, watching Justin pull something from his pocket. "I've seen the proof. And I think we should get married."

Her mouth dropped. For a second she was glad he was holding on to her as his announcement sent her reeling.

"You *what?*"

"I'll admit I'm flying by the seat of my pants here," Justin's gaze flickered from her to her family, then came back, reflecting hesitation but also a strong sense of purpose. "But I will not miss out on one day of being a father. Not this time. Not with this baby."

This was crazy! She yanked from his touch. "There is no baby."

"You'll be a wonderful stepmother for Jacoby," Justin continued speaking over her protest. "The cabin isn't very big, but I'm sure Gage won't mind if I add another room. It's plain and practical at the moment, but I know you can make it a home…for all of us, for our family."

All the right words for all the wrong reasons.

Gina had dreamed that one day Justin would ask her to share his life, but not this way. He didn't love her. He was running on pure adrenaline after all he'd been through and the idea that their time together had created a baby had him teetering on the edge of an imaginary cliff.

"There will be no wedding," Gina stated firmly, tearing her gaze from him to look at her brother and then her mother. The shocked expression on her pale face caused Gina's stomach to take a nauseous roll. Wow, losing her dinner on Justin's boots wouldn't help her make her case.

She pulled in a deep breath and tried again. "I. Am. Not. Pregnant."

"She's right. I am."

Everyone turned to look at Racy. She walked to Justin and pulled the stick from his grip. "This pregnancy test is mine."

Turning to her husband, she smiled. "I'm the one who's going to have a baby."

"You are? We are?" Gage stammered. "But how— Why would Jacoby think—"

"I took the test today at Gina's." Racy laid a hand on her husband's chest, moving closer as he encircled her in his arms. "I've been waiting for the best time to tell you, but things have been a bit hectic tonight."

"But…it's us?" Gage asked.

"Yes." Racy rose on tiptoe and gave her husband a quick kiss. "It's us, Daddy."

Gage's smile was wide as he wrapped Racy in a bear hug, but he immediately released her to lay a hand over her still-flat belly. Racy covered his hand with hers and nodded.

Gina turned away, blinking back the sting of tears at the loving gesture.

"Oh, this is wonderful news!" Sandy Steele clasped her hands together. "Let's all go inside and celebrate! I've got freshly baked pies cooling in the kitchen."

Gina sent her a grateful look, silently mouthing *thank you* as her mother hustled everyone back into the house, including Jacoby, who seemed just as happy his title was now cousin instead of big brother.

Silence fell over the yard again, as uncomfortable as before because she wasn't alone out there. Justin hadn't moved a step either.

With a jolt of awareness, Gina realized she never said a word of good wishes to her brother. "I didn't even congratulate Gage."

"Me neither," Justin said. "Congratulate either of them, I mean."

"Boy, from parents to aunt and uncle in a heartbeat."

Her words sounded pathetic, but Gina felt powerless to stop them as they tumbled from her mouth. She cast a sideways look in Justin's direction. The stunned expression in his eyes was mixed with a hint of—

Disappointment? No, that couldn't be right.

She turned to him. "Why did you ever think I was pregnant?"

"Jacoby found the test stick in your bathroom and he heard you and Racy talking." He closed his eyes for a moment, then opened them to look at her. "He said you were excited…he thought it was you…"

"And you assumed I was keeping the possibility of a child from you."

Justin nodded. "Gina, I'm so—"

"Don't say it." She cut him off, putting more space between them. "I don't need your apology."

She couldn't do this. She couldn't stand here and listen to him express regret over the sweet words he'd spoken, because deep inside, she truly wanted everything Justin offered her.

Except he forgot to include one thing, the part of himself she needed the most.

His heart.

"I wish you luck with Jacoby." She started walking backward toward the deck. "Like I said before, you two belong together. I hope his grandparents or the judge—whoever you have to convince—can see that."

"Gina—"

Her feet hit the steps and she stumbled. Justin reached out, but she righted herself before he could touch her. She scooted up the stairs, not stopping until she grabbed the door handle. "I'm going inside for a piece of pie and to celebrate with everyone. You should come in, too."

Justin joined her with a hollow laugh, each step slow and measured. "Yeah. A celebration. Just what I'm in the mood for."

Chapter Sixteen

"What do you mean Gina's leaving town?"

"She told us a few days ago at the library." Jacoby looked up from where he lay on the cabin's living room floor, a large poster board in front of him. He carefully lifted the paint-brush and he filled in the block letters drawn on the poster with bright red paint. "I told you, but you were busy looking at a bunch of papers. She's going away to school."

Stunned, Justin glanced over at his sister who stood pouring herself a glass of iced tea at the center island in his kitchen. Racy nodded, confirming his son's words.

"I don't want her to go," Jacoby continued. "None of us do. It was hard to say goodbye to her. That's why we decided to carry these signs on the library float in the parade tomorrow. To show her how much we love her and thank her for the stories she's read to us."

Jacoby went back to work on his sign. The late-May afternoon sun streamed through the window, drying the letters he'd already finished.

Still processing the news, Justin walked into his kitchen to grab a soda from the refrigerator.

"You didn't know?"

Racy's softly voiced question caused Justin to look at her again. He opened the can and took a long draw from it before answering her. "No, but I can tell from the expression on your face you did."

She nodded. "On the same crazy day you decided the best way to handle the news of a possible baby was to suggest a shotgun wedding, she told me she planned to go back to school—away from Destiny."

"A shotgun wedding, huh? Like the good sheriff would've allowed anything else if she really had been pregnant." Justin slumped to the kitchen counter next to his sister and pressed the cold can to his forehead.

"Well, I thought it was sweet."

"Sweet?" Justin lowered the can and glanced over his shoulder at Jacoby to make sure he wasn't listening. "Gina hates me now thanks to my big mouth."

Racy put down her glass of iced tea and laid a hand on Justin's arm. "Oh, honey, please don't think that way. She doesn't hate you. That's the last thing she feels. She—"

Justin looked at his sister when she cut off her own words. "She...what?"

Racy shook her head and offered a gentle squeeze. "Sorry, big brother, but you're on your own figuring that one out. Not that you've had much time to think about her feelings or even your own when it comes to the two of you. I know it's been a demanding week for you."

Demanding was exactly right. It'd been a hell of a week.

Justin had spent Monday in three separate meetings. First with a lawyer recommended by Jennifer Steele, then with Jacoby's doctor and then with the Ellsworths.

In that order.

He'd filed the paperwork requesting physical custody of

Jacoby and things were looking good for the request to go through without any issues, considering the Ellsworths had agreed with the idea.

Jacoby's grandparents had decided they didn't want to use the loss of their daughter to cause another parent to be separated from his child.

They asked for visitations and Justin had agreed, promising to bring Jacoby to see them at least once a month. From there, they could work their way up to the boy spending longer periods of time with his grandparents.

"Yeah, demanding," Justin agreed when he noticed his sister seemed to be waiting for a reply. "But, geez, I must've really been out of it not to hear my son tell me that Gina was packing her bags and getting out of Dodge."

"Maybe she doesn't think she has any reason to stay," Racy said with a smile. "Yes, her family is here, but they'll always be her family no matter where she is. She doesn't have a job and volunteering at the library is what fueled her desire to be a teacher."

"A teacher?"

Racy nodded. "She's going back to school to get her teaching credentials in elementary education."

Justin couldn't believe it. After she'd put that idea in his head a few weeks ago, she was now taking her own advice. Gina would be an awesome teacher, she had a natural gentleness with kids Jacoby's age. She didn't talk down to them or make what they had to say seem unimportant.

He'd actually found himself on the website for the University of Wyoming, looking at their College of Education. Becoming a teacher himself was still just a dream, but he'd enjoyed working on a scared-straight type of program for teens while in prison. Maybe he could start off being a temporary and work his way up.

"Justin? Did I lose you again?"

"Huh?" He snapped out of his thoughts to find his sister grabbing her purse and coat. "Ah, when is Gina leaving?"

"Tomorrow after the Memorial Day parade."

"Tomorrow?" His heart seized in his chest, waiting a full heartbeat before it resumed an unsteady pounding. "Why so soon?"

"She's hoping to get into a summer session."

Racy gave him a quick kiss and headed for the door. Justin walked with her, waiting as she stopped to give Jacoby a goodbye kiss, as well, then followed her out to her car.

"If you've got something to tell her, I think you better do it today," she said, climbing behind the wheel. "Before it's too late."

He waited until she put on her seat belt and started down the road before he headed back to the porch, his sister's words ringing in his head. Talk to Gina? She'd made it clear she wasn't interested in anything he had to say, but he couldn't let her leave town without her knowing—

Knowing what?

How much it meant to him that she'd believed in him from the very beginning, standing up for him when no one would? How she'd been by his side from the moment his son appeared and never let Justin's doubts and inner demons get in the way of what he had to do to keep Jacoby safe and happy? How she'd taught him to laugh, to think, to dream?

How she'd changed his life?

"Hey, Dad!"

He opened the screen door and went back inside. "What do you need, Jacoby?"

"Is love spelled with an *o* or a *u?*"

Justin smiled.

Neither. In his eyes, his heart and deep in his soul, he knew he would forever spell it G-i-n-a.

"It's an *o*," he said. "L-o-v-e. Why?"

"I want to make another sign." Jacoby leaned over a fresh

piece of poster board. "Everyone is saying thank you or how happy she makes us, but I want to make a sign that says 'We Love You,' even though I like l-u-v-e better."

He crouched beside his son. "Why do you want to say that?"

Jacoby looked up at him. "Because we do. Love her. Right? So why not just say it?"

Justin dropped to his knees and reached for a paintbrush. Why not, indeed?

Gina clapped along with everyone else lining Main Street when the high school marching band led off the annual Memorial Day parade as the church bells chimed the noon hour.

The weather was so warm that she wore the strapless sundress and wedge sandals she'd purchased while on vacation. Everyone around her was also dressed for the heat, so she didn't feel out of place. Here she was, finally feeling like a part of this town and a part of her family, and she was leaving again.

Her mother's hand landed lightly on her shoulder. "Here come the twins."

They watched Gage's precious vintage pickup, decked out in school colors and filled with members of the senior class, cruise down the street. Although the vehicle was barely crawling due to the speed of the parade, Garrett looked nervous behind the wheel. Giselle had been chosen as one of the class princesses and shone again in her senior prom finery.

Gina sighed. The twins had tried to persuade her to stick around for a few more weeks, at least until their graduation, but she promised to come back for the ceremony and party.

She couldn't stay. Not for one more day.

If she did, she was sure she would end up on Justin's front porch, again, only this time she'd spill out her heart and make a fool of herself—to a man who'd made it clear he wasn't interested.

Unless, of course, she was pregnant and he was forced to do something about it.

"I wonder if Gage has seen what they've done to his truck," Racy said, joining them. "Good thing I've got airline tickets and hotel arrangements to distract him."

Gina scooted over to make room for her sister-in-law. "Are you talking about your Paris honeymoon?"

"Yes, we're finally going. We head out a few days after the twins graduate. Then it's two full weeks in the most romantic city in the world." Racy sighed and patted her belly. "I can't wait, even if I can't sample any of the French wines."

"Where is Gage?"

"He's working the parade route, but we'll probably run into him later at the fairgrounds for the barbecue. You are coming, right? Before you head out?"

Gina's car was packed and ready to go. She was driving as far as Hastings, Nebraska, tonight with plans to continue to South Bend and the Notre Dame campus in the morning.

"I don't know. It's a six-hour drive to my hotel. I should head out as soon as the parade ends."

Yes, she was avoiding the town-wide picnic because she'd probably run into Justin and Jacoby. It was going to be hard enough to stand here and watch the library float go by and wave to the little boy. She knew the story-hour kids were being featured. She'd been asked to sit on the float, too, but she begged off.

More groups came by. The 4-H crowd featured every kind of animal from horses to sheep, and the local square dancing troupe do-si-doed and walked at the same time, the ladies' colorful skirts swirling. The military veterans came next, some fresh from the Middle East, others dressed in uniforms decades old, marching with a local National Guard unit and flag detail. In an instant, the crowd was on its feet, showing appreciation of their service with loud applause.

Then she saw the library float.

Because of the ages of the children on board, the float was on a lowboy trailer, only two feet off the ground and being pulled by a slow-moving tractor. A short railing made sure no one could tumble off by accident and colorful fringe wrapped around three sides. The dozen or so kids and members of the library staff sat in a field of green grass with flowers made of construction and tissue paper to look like books.

The boys and girls were waving to the crowd and held up signs, but they were still too far away to read. As they got closer, Gina could finally make out the words. Joy burst forth from deep inside her.

Thank you, Gina!

Gina + Reading = Fun!

Smile If U Luv 2 Read!

"Oh, the signs are wonderful." Her mother reached for her hand and gave her a gentle squeeze. "How sweet!"

"Those kids really love you."

Gina turned at the sound of Gage's voice, surprised to find him standing next to Racy. Seconds later, Giselle and Garrett joined them.

"Whew, we made it in time," Giselle said.

Garrett faked handing the keys to Gage's truck to him with a wide grin and pocketed them instead. "Yeah, we didn't want to miss this."

"Miss what?" Gina looked at her family.

Gage gently turned her around to face the parade again, the tractor having slowed to a stop right in front of where Gina stood with her family.

Then she saw the black Stetson.

And the man wearing it.

Dressed in a white button-down shirt, snug-fitting jeans and cowboy boots, he climbed off the back of the float.

Justin.

Her heart lodged in her throat, making her work twice as hard to breathe. She watched him gently lift each of the children, one by one, from the float. They ran toward where she stood on the sidewalk, each holding a yellow rose in their hands.

Tears gathered in her eyes as she accepted each rose and a hug from the boys and girls who then ran back to the float and climbed aboard again.

Except for one boy and one man.

Jacoby stood next to his father in a matching outfit, from the miniature black Stetson to the cowboy boots. They each grabbed a sign in one hand and a yellow rose in the other and slowly walked toward her as the parade continued on its way.

We love you, Gina, read the sign Jacoby carried.

The simple block letters on Justin's spelled out, *With all our hearts.*

Gina brushed away her tears, surprised at how much she wanted to believe those words meant…something. She warned herself not to get her hopes up, her fingers clenching the roses in her hand. She'd never wanted anything in her life as much as she wanted to believe the smile on Justin's face and the confidence in his gaze as he stopped in front of her.

"This is for you." Jacoby held out the rose.

Gina bent down to take the flower and then gave Jacoby a big hug. "You look so grown-up. I love your hat."

"Thanks! Do you like our signs?"

She straightened and touched the edge of the poster board. "Yes, I do, very much."

"They were my dad's idea."

Looking up, she found Justin watching her. "They were?"

"Yes, they were." He rested his sign at his feet and handed

over the last rose to her. When her fingers brushed his, he wrapped her hand in his, his thumb tracing back and over her knuckles.

"Gina, I want to thank you—"

"Thank me?"

He took a step closer, raised her hand to his lips and gently placed a kiss there. "Let me finish, okay? I want to thank you for loving Jacoby and for loving me."

Stunned, Gina could only stand there and stare at him.

Justin's smile faded as his gaze turned serious. "I've always thought I had nothing to offer. My past mistakes were something I couldn't erase and those mistakes make me feel worthless. If it hadn't been for you I would've never believed I could be anything else. You never gave up on me, you never let me give up on Jacoby and you made me see that a person is defined by who they are now, not what they once did. I want to start a family with Jacoby, but I don't want to do it alone."

He dug his hand into his pocket and pulled out a ring. "I know a marriage proposal is a bit impulsive considering I haven't even asked you out on an official date yet, but I'd like you to wear this, on your right hand, as a promise of my love and how much I want…we want you in our lives. I do love you, Gina. With all my heart."

Gina's fingers shook as Justin slid the delicate art deco and filigree diamond ring on her finger. "Justin, it's beautiful."

"And if you still have to go away to find your dream—" Justin paused and silenced Jacoby's protest with a look "—we want you to know we'll be right here waiting when you get back."

"I don't have to go anywhere," Gina answered, pouring all of her love for this man and his little boy into her words. "I can work on getting my teaching credentials in Cheyenne. I'm staying right here because I love you, too, both of you, with all of my heart."

She heard Jacoby's squeal of delight and her family's cheers, but all she felt was the love and strength of Justin's arms as he pulled her to him and lowered his mouth to hers in a kiss that held the promise of tomorrow, the promise of forever.

* * * * *

Special Offers

Every month we put together collections and longer reads written by your favourite authors.

Here are some of next month's highlights—and don't miss our fabulous discount online!

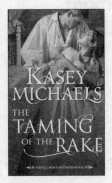

On sale 18th May

On sale 1st June

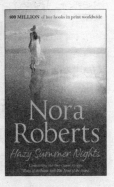

On sale 1st June

Save 20%
on all Special Releases

MILLS & BOON Book Club

2 Free Books!

Get your free books now at
www.millsandboon.co.uk/freebookoffer

Or fill in the form below and post it back to us

THE MILLS & BOON® BOOK CLUB™—HERE'S HOW IT WORKS: Accepting your free books places you under no obligation to buy anything. You may keep the books and return the despatch note marked 'Cancel'. If we do not hear from you, about a month later we'll send you 5 brand-new stories from the Cherish™ series, including two 2-in-1 books priced at £5.49 each, and a single book priced at £3.49*. There is no extra charge for post and packaging. You may cancel at any time, otherwise we will send you 5 stories a month which you may purchase or return to us—the choice is yours. *Terms and prices subject to change without notice. Offer valid in UK only. Applicants must be 18 or over. Offer expires 31st July 2012. **For full terms and conditions, please go to www.millsandboon.co.uk/freebookoffer**

Mrs/Miss/Ms/Mr (please circle)
_____

First Name
_____

Surname
_____

Address
_____

_____

                                    Postcode
_____

E-mail
_____

Send this completed page to: Mills & Boon Book Club, Free Book Offer, FREEPOST NAT 10298, Richmond, Surrey, TW9 1BR

Find out more at
www.millsandboon.co.uk/freebookoffer

Visit us Online

0112/S2XEA/REV

The World of Mills & Boon®

There's a Mills & Boon® series that's perfect for you. We publish ten series and with new titles every month, you never have to wait long for your favourite to come along.

Blaze. Scorching hot, sexy reads

By Request Relive the romance with the best of the best

Cherish Romance to melt the heart every time

Desire Passionate and dramatic love stories